NIGHT SHIFT

Stories from the Life of an ER Doc

NIGHT SHIFT

Stories from the Life of an ER Doc

MARK PLASTER, MD

WITH A FOREWORD BY **GREG HENRY, MD**

NIGHT SHIFT

Copyright © 2013 Mark Plaster

All rights reserved. Except as permitted under U.S. Copyright Act of 1976, no part of this publication may be reproduced, distributed, or transmitted in any form or by any means, or stored in a database or retrieval system, without the prior written permission of the publisher.

The information contained in this book is not intended to serve as a replacement for professional medical advice. Any use of the information in this book is at the reader's discretion. The author and publisher specifically disclaim any and all liability arising directly or indirectly from the use or application of any information contained in this book. A health care professional should be consulted regarding your specific situation.

M. L. Plaster Publishing Co., LLC
4794 Bayfields Road
Harwood, MD 20776

Visit our website at www.epmonthly.com.

ISBN: 978-1-940328-00-3

Printed in the United States of America

Book design by Elise Grinstead of Elisign Design
Cover design by Logan Plaster

First Edition: October 2013

10 9 8 7 6 5 4 3 2 1

This book is dedicated to my loving wife, Rebecca, who always demanded to know what I was doing every night I was away from her.

CONTENTS

Foreword..ix
Introduction..xv

SECTION I. *Discovering the Night*

1. Discovering the Night..3
2. Bat Bite on Butt..9
3. An Easy Decision...13
4. What Goes Around...19
5. Take a Deep Breath...23
6. My Mona Lisa..27
7. Slap of Life...31
8. A Legend in His Own Mind....................................35
9. Innocence Lost..39
10. Tricks and Treats...43
11. Image is Everything, Almost...................................47
12. Triage..51
13. Friendly Fire..57
14. Science and Art...63
15. Discomfort Zones...67
16. Terror..73
17. Sick Day..79
18. Betrayal..83
19. Nuts...87
20. Exit Strategy..93

SECTION II. *In the Desert*

21. I Want YOU...101
22. Nothing to Fear, But... 105
23. Drill..109

24. In the Desert...113
25. Hurry Up and Wait...117
26. For Such a Time as This..121
27. Father's Day.. 127
28. The Economy of Gratitude.. 131

SECTION III. *Answering The Call*

29. The Colonel... 139
30. Survivor's Guilt..145
31. In the Middle..149
32. Answering the Call.. 153
33. Finger Pointing... 159
34. Dumbfounded...163
35. Do-It-Yourselfer..169
36. Geezer...175
37. Hero... 179
38. Homicide..183
39. Just Keeping Up.. 187
40. One at a Time...191
41. Therapy Session.. 195
42. Wedding Bell Blues... 199
43. Square One...203
44. Telemedicine...209
45. Show Me.. 213
46. History Lesson..219
47. Conspiracy Theory..225
48. Aphephobia..229

Acknowledgments...233

FOREWORD

A Quest for Meaning

THE FIRST QUESTION YOU SHOULD ASK is why does a book need a foreword? Parenthetically, a book by an emergency doctor about emergency medicine should not need a foreword. Just get down and dirty and start the book already! But this book that "moves the meat" with a move-the-meat attitude requires some advanced preparation.

Don't get me wrong: I like Mark Plaster. But what is it specifically that makes me want to read Mark Plaster, which I do every month? If I want a review of current scientific thinking on a subject, I'll read a column by Jim Roberts or Rick Bukata. No, scientific analysis is not the answer. So is it his Hemingway-style prose? Not really. Many authors in emergency medicine spew terse comments like bullets from a machine gun.

As I sat thinking about my mission to compose a foreword, I was in the midst of my tenth or eleventh re-reading of Viktor Frankl's *Man's Search for Meaning* when it hit me square in the face that I read Mark to commiserate with another emergency doctor about what one's life in medicine means. Its turmoil. Its trouble. Its unhappiness. (For those of you not familiar with Frankl's work, let me just say that he was a Jewish prisoner of the Nazis. Things don't get much worse.)

But as emergency doctors, we understand chaos if nothing else. Dr. Plaster's *Night Shift* has been, over these many years, an attempt to find a pathway to understand the 'why' in what we do for a living. Science can never be the answer, but only a methodology and a fact-base for looking at problems. But only value judgments can give us a sense of whether we have done good or bad, right or wrong.

Mark has been the Virgil to my Dante, taking me on a journey (which is by no means over) through both physical and psychological hell. Mark has allowed us to walk with him as he peered into the bulges of the descent.

What the *Night Shift* stories bring to all of us who have been doing emergency medicine—either as a doctor, a nurse, an EMT, physician assistant, nurse practitioner, or tech—is a touch-point in reality. This is an author who has been there and done that. He has the t-shirt and has paid his dues. He sees the world not from fifty thousand feet but from the five feet between the intoxicated patient's fist and our collective noses. You get the sense that Mark has lived on cold pizza, had to beg attendings to do what is right, and silently wept in private after giving back a dead child to devastated parents.

We understand Mark because he is *us*. Emergency people don't trust and can't relate to those who have not been confronted by and managed human tragedy. It is an enormous world, but humans live in small communities of a few people who really matter to each other. The great shifts in world politics and economic maelstroms have almost no import on the mind of someone watching their parent or spouse dying in front of them. This is where emergency people live: not as socialists or capitalists, not as Christians or Muslims or Jews, but as one tightly knit group of people helping individuals make it through the night. It is often not the living or the dying, but the tender word or gesture that makes all the difference to those who are forced to enter our doors.

Dante reminds us in the intense terza rima of the *Inferno* that over the gates of hell is written, "Abandon all hope, ye who enter here." It is our job to provide more than technical excellence; it is our job to offer human kindness and hope. We cure sometimes, manage mostly, but we can always care. The doors to the emergency department are the very antithesis of the gates of hell.

To read this collection of *Night Shift* is to recapitulate our phylogeny as a specialty, our embryonic beginnings, born out of a need to look at the world not as what we'd like it to be, but as it actually is.

First, we, like all religions and philosophies, went through an axial period where our concepts, foundations, and beliefs were set. The world's first axial period lasted from about 800 BCE to 300 BCE. Emergency medicine experienced a similar period wherein, from about 1965 to 1975, emergency rooms with rotating doctors of every specialty (under what is called the Pontiac Plan) metamorphasized rapidly to involve doctors dedicated to emergency medicine (under the Alexandria model). With the founding of ACEP in 1968 and the first Scientific Assembly in 1969 (attended by 250 people), the stakes were in the ground to define the landscape of a new order of emergency care.

In my youth ambulances were run mostly by funeral homes, which constitutes the most obvious conflict of interests ever seen. The meteoric rise of residencies, from just one in 1972 to 162 today, combined with the creation of academic departments of emergency medicine, board certification and superiority in educational programs, allowed us to take our place among other specialties, knowing that the best and brightest medical students of today are joining us in the ranks of emergency medicine.

The story of the end of the twentieth century and the beginning of this new millennium is the story of the expansion of modernity with its glut of technology and capital funding. All this knowledge of high tech should be viewed as a marvel, but not a miracle. This elevation to a global village brings conflicting ideas face-to-face with no neutral arbiter of truth. How do we combine all these forces to construct practice patterns in medicine that relate five thousand years of values and two thousand years of beliefs to the rapidly moving times in which we live? Pluralism and uncertainty have been on a headlong collision course with belief since the days of Martin Luther and the council of Trent.

In the United States these ideas are about to explode. Subjectivism and relativism have replaced belief. "It's all relative, man," has become our mantra. We have abandoned Aristotle's four causes. It has been proclaimed that fact is king and values are evil, because they force us to make value judgments and who are we to judge? 'How-questions' control the world; 'why-questions' are verboten. In the gospel of John we encounter the concept of Logos, 'the Word.' Are we just a genetic code, or is there a soul? Is it the four dimensions, or is there a fifth dimension? Each practitioner must answer these questions in order to have a coherent basis on which to proceed with care. We each need a telos, a purpose to prevent us from Charlie Chaplin's dilemma in *Modern Times*. We are not truly being individuals if we are not truly unique individuals. And if we have not recognized our potential for fulfilling experiences and living meaningfully, then should we expect anything at all?

What I now realize is that Mark Plaster has been asking and answering these questions all along. As you read the various vignettes, keep in mind that it is the interactions with patients that keep us human. Pride is/was the sin of Lucifer, and we fly dangerously close to the sun every time we take undue credit for medical success. As you progress through the chapters, keep in mind also the Manichean battles of good and evil, right and wrong, which are value-based. Saint Augustine said the doctrines of life are set in two books: the book of Nature, i.e. Science, which fields objective truth, while the book of Scripture, i.e. Faith, speaks of theology as not a single religion but as a force of creation and purpose. *Fides et ratio,* faith and reason, are both needed to practice medicine. To have one without the other does not work. There are instruction manuals for every cancer radiation therapy machine in the world; there is no manual as to whether a patient's life will be made better or worse with the application of such therapy. There are treatises on how to resuscitate a child; there really is no book to inform you how to tell a parent that the child they love is dead and that your heart is breaking along with theirs.

Science is, in some ways, the ancilla to philosophy; it tries to tell us what heaven might be made of, but it can never tell us how to get there.

Mark's insights and snippets into the medical experience never ask the proof of the Big Bang theory of George Lemaître. Most people don't realize that Lemaître was both a physicist and a Jesuit priest. Our current (almost universal) acceptance of the Big Bang creation and the expanding universe presumes the existence of a creator. Mark really never says so, but I like to think that he possesses a creator and an immortal soul. And how else can you explain our virtual cheering in triumph and our sobbing quietly with loss?

Joseph Campbell, a social scientist with whom I am often at philosophical odds, claimed one thing with which I must agree: A quest is the center and source of all mythology as it is our own lives.

This book is the antidote for postmodernism where nothing means anything at all. Openness to the point of total nihilism is crazy, leading to total indifference. I reject this view of the world, and as you are soon to see, so does Dr. Plaster.

Thank you, Mark; for reminding us of who we are and that we're still human. *Gaudeamus igitur.*

—Greg Henry, MD
August 2013

INTRODUCTION

IT WAS IN THE LATE EIGHTIES when I began writing the stories in *Night Shift*. And, as with most worthwhile things in my life, they began at my wife's request. I had just returned home from working a night shift, and, as usual, I was eating breakfast and talking to Rebecca before the kids got up and I headed to bed. "We have to talk," she said, pulling up a chair to the table. That was usually the beginning of something that ended with me begging forgiveness. "The principal called me aside yesterday and told me that Graham [our oldest son] is telling the other kids that you can raise people from the dead. They thought it was pretty funny, but thought you might tone down the hero worship a little."

"Really?" I knew my son had an imagination, but...

"It turns out that what actually happened was that an ambulance came by while the kids were on the playground and Graham casually told everyone that somebody had probably died and they were taking them to the hospital for his daddy to bring them back to life."

"Oh," I said, going back to my munching. "What's wrong with that?"

"Nothing, except that's all he thinks you do all night. Why don't you write down some of the things that you see in the ER. I'm sure that even if they can't appreciate it now, they will someday."

I thought about it and, as is usually the case, she was right. I realized that every night tragedies and comedies, great and small, were played out in front of me. As I sat down to write about my experiences, I would find myself weeping, laughing, or just shaking my head in amazement at the stream of life that I had witnessed the night before. Writing became my own post-traumatic stress therapy when I recalled having to tell a mother who had accidentally backed her car over her two-year-old daughter that, contrary to my son's belief, we could not bring her little girl back to life. Fiction became easier to tell than the truth as I recalled the elderly man with the Christmas tree-shaped lightbulb stuck in his rectum swearing to me that his doctor recommended it as a treatment for his hemorrhoids. The stories, like life and death, just kept coming night after night.

If you are an emergency physician, married to an emergency physician, or simply know an emergency physician, you've probably heard some of these stories before. Because these are the stories of every ER doc, nurse, paramedic, technician, or orderly who has worked while the rest of the world slept. Every year over 130 million patients go through the doors of an ER. So while some of our stories may sound like urban legends, there's probably a good-sized nugget of truth in every one.

But there are some unique aspects to my perspective on this experience. First, my career started at the very beginning of emergency medicine as a specialty. 1979, the year that I graduated from the School of Medicine at the University of Missouri-Columbia, was the first year that physicians could take a specialty-certifying exam in emergency medicine. The field was so new that my advisors attempted to talk me out of pursuing a career in what they presumed would be an eternal internship. And at first they were right. When I reported to Akron General Medical Center for training, I soon found that we were treated as the eternal interns, taking every other or every third night call with the interns on every specialty we covered. For three years, my wife and children virtually never saw me awake. They would come to the hospital to join me for dinner in the cafeteria. I got so tired of patients asking what I was going to do when I got out of internship that I grew a beard just to look older and wiser.

But over the next decade the specialty grew exponentially in responsibility and respect. Soon the demand for board certified EPs so far exceeded the supply that every ER was short staffed, especially at night. And that's when I decided to pursue a career as a full-time locum tenens physician. I became a full-time temp. Whether it was in Texas, Michigan, North Carolina, or Hawaii, I would fly in on the day of my first shift, work up to fourteen consecutive twelve-hour night shifts and then fly home. There was no end to the work. I could have worked every night of my life if I'd had the energy. As it was, I logged a combined total of thirteen years of time awake at night and over four million miles on American Airlines. At one time I had fourteen different state licenses. When I went to a new emergency department I wanted to know four things; where's the bathroom, where do I pick up the charts of patients to be seen, who are the "problem children" on the medical staff, and where's the coffee pot. And I needed that information in reverse order.

About halfway through these stories you will also discover another oddity about my career in emergency medicine. At age forty-nine, after twenty-three years in emergency medicine, I became inspired by my son at the US Naval Academy to join the Navy Reserve. I wanted to serve my country like all the other men in my family. Besides it seemed like a fun thing to do; I thought that wearing a cool uniform might even turn my wife on. But two months after I had agreed to one weekend drill a month and two weeks training in the summer, the twin towers fell on September 11th. As my wife and I sat on the couch witnessing the horror, we both knew this was going to effect us personally. It was only a matter of months before I found myself wearing body armor and seated between two young men with .50 caliber machine guns as we flew a CH53 helicopter over the Iraqi border. With little more than a couple weeks of military training I became the officer in charge of Shock Trauma Platoon Seven, United States Marine Corps. I probably would have soiled my pants that day if I could have relaxed my butt muscles enough.

It was a time of testing for me. ER docs are not known for taking orders from anyone. I was an old dog and this was a new trick. I could take hot, but this was 135 degrees. I had eaten from vending machines for years, but I found that MRE (Meals Ready to Eat) really meant Meals Resistant to Excretion. I lost twenty-five pounds without even trying. I had argued so relentlessly with my wife over the previous twenty-five years that I'm sure she had considered both murder and divorce, simultaneously; but I came to miss her so much that I would weep over her letters.

And then there were the boys. Young men of course, for they were doing the heavy lifting for the peace of our world. But these marines were the ages of my children. I ran into one young man that I had coached in fifth grade basketball camp. I treated the limbs that were nearly blown off, the eyes that were shot out, and, of course, pronounced and prayed over the dead. People often say, "Oh you were in a MASH unit," referring to the famous TV show. But I explain, "You know in the opening scene of *MASH,* where the helicopters are flying in with the wounded? I was the guy who was sending them back from the front lines." Returning home I found my wife was either ten years younger or I was ten years older. My children had babies. And CNN was at my house to talk to "the grandfather who went to war." All I knew was that everything in the world had changed. Everything, of course, except the stream of life that flowed through the emergency department every night.

In a strange way, getting back to the chaos and cacophony of a night shift was very comforting to me. This was home. These were my people. And these were my stories.

But there is one thing you must understand; all these stories are fictionalized. Not pure fiction, mind you, because I could never make some of this up. But if you have been one of the more than 125,000 patients that I treated over the last thirty years and you think a story is about you, it probably is not. To do less would be a violation of privacy that I would never consider. The patients, doctors, and nurses in these stories are all composites of people I've known. For in those thirty years, I have seen every imaginable situation at least a half dozen times.

So if you are an ER doc like me, or just someone who is fascinated by stories of the thousands of people who hold up the safety net of society night after night, try this: wait until about three in the morning, get a cold cup of coffee and a stale doughnut, and come join me for a night in the ER. There are a lot more stories where these came from.

SECTION I
Discovering the Night

1

Discovering the Night

FOR MANY YEARS I TRIED in every way I could to avoid working nights. But to no avail. It was my lot in life. If I had thought about the fact that fully one-half of my professional career would be spent working while others are sleeping, it might have given me second thoughts about entering the field of emergency medicine. But I did discover something worse than night shifts...rotating shifts. Just when you got your body adjusted to one shift you changed to another. Regular or irregular rotations, it's all the same. It was torture shifting my body clock. So after years of listening to everyone complain, I offered to try something: full-time nights. Twelve-hour shifts made it doable for the family. And by doing the unspeakable six shifts in a row, I would get eight days off out of every two weeks. It was still painful to shift from night to day, but I only did it twice a fortnight.

More importantly, however, I discovered a new world. A world where no drug reps or administrators called. A world where the coffee was strong and the doughnuts were stale. The cafeteria was closed. In place of a suit and tie, wrinkled scrubs and a five o'clock shadow were expected. Most of the trauma cases came in at night. But you also got the babies. And I love babies.

Here's a typical night. A young couple brought in their four-day-old girl. Picking up the chart I noticed that the parents complained that their baby was making funny noises and seemed to have difficulty breathing. Respiratory distress in a newborn is a serious issue, so I rushed into the room expecting the worst. What I found was a peacefully sleeping baby, a truly beautiful little girl, the glowing picture of health. When I went to pick her up I noticed a videotape next to her on the bed. Asking what it was for, the young father, a very tech savvy sort, told me that he had taken a video of her in distress so that I could understand better.

"Wow, that's great," I said. "I seldom get to witness the actual event. I have a player in my office that we use for educational videos. Let's go see it. Maybe there will be some clues as to what's wrong."

As we went to the office my mind was sorting through possible scenarios...a momentary airway obstruction, a brief seizure, possibly even an apneic episode, signaling a risk for SIDS. I inserted the tape and watched as the baby grunted, puckered her lips, and strained until her face turned crimson. Then it was over and she looked fine.

"How long ago did you take this video?" I asked.

"Oh, just minutes before we rushed in," he replied. I walked back to the bedside with the parents in tow and peeked into her diaper.

"I have some good news for you," I said. "She pooped. And that's a good thing." I didn't have the heart to tell them what that first stool cost in medical bills—at least they had it on video.

Next, as I usually do when I am trying to save time, I picked up several charts at once and walked into the first exam room. Seated in the corner was a man in his late twenties with a three-year-old boy on his lap. The bed, however, was empty. Both had rigid expressions that I took to be anxiety. It was not uncommon in my experience for a child to fear leaving the safety of a parent's lap. The ER bed, with its starched sheet, seemed so foreboding. As I introduced myself, neither the boy nor his father moved a muscle. I thought I might have to pry the little guy off his dad's lap. But when I looked at the chart, the name on it was that of a woman. Thinking that I had walked into the wrong room, I started to leave and apologized. "I'm sorry, I'm in the wrong room. I thought a woman was in this room."

Finally, as if exhaling, the dad said, "You're looking for my wife. She's in X-ray." Immediately, the youngster spun around and pointed his finger at his dad's face. "You lose! You lose!" The defeated father explained that they were playing 'the quiet game' and that his son was very competitive. It soon became apparent why the father had kept the game going. Once the floodgates were open, the little guy couldn't stop talking.

"He's a big talker," his father said with resignation.

"Really," was all I could say. The boy told me he was five (he was three), that he had a little sister (he was an only child), and that he had a dog and cat (they were only stuffed animals). But he was convincing of each. Anything I asked his father, and eventually his mother, he answered in great detail, most of it fabrication. The x-rays and exam of the mother were normal, so she was discharged without delay. But her son was still talking as they all left the department. As they passed the nurses' station the staff just looked at the mother with sympathy.

"Can you imagine being in that household?" one finally said. "It would make the ER seem peaceful."

"I think that's why she came," said the charge nurse.

The next chart looked like a fairly simple complaint. "Superficial burns to the hands and legs," read the nurse's note. I was always amazed by the simple complaints that came to the emergency department at the oddest hours. But I never complained because it was good to be able to get ahead with a few quick cases. It never failed that we would have a rush of patients just as all the extra staff was leaving. And once it started getting backed up I'd hear the same complaint, "It's about time you got here!" So, after a perfunctory introduction I jumped right into the exam. The burns were superficial to the hands and legs with some blistering. No full thickness burns or circumferential burns. Less than 1 percent total body surface area. I was taking notes as fast as I could. I barely saw the man's face. Pretty straightforward, I thought. Finally I looked up to ask the patient how he was tolerating the pain.

"I'm fine," the stately elderly man mumbled.

"How did this happen?" I asked, as if it was an afterthought. The patient raised his gaze to meet mine for the first time and then burst into uncontrollable sobbing.

"It was all my fault," he said dropping his face into his hands. "I fell asleep at the wheel of my new RV and drove it off the road. It rolled on its side and caught fire." His body convulsed with his weeping.

I began checking him further for other injuries that could have been sustained in the wreck. "But your wounds are minor," I finally said, trying to reassure him. "And your RV can be replaced."

He raised his face to meet mine once more.

"My two precious granddaughters were in the back, asleep," he whispered. "I couldn't get them out. I tried..." he sobbed. "But I couldn't get them."

I had no medicine in my arsenal for the pain that he felt. All I could do was drop to my knees in front of his chair and hold him in my arms to keep him from collapsing to the floor. Thoughts of a fiery crash, this poor man's deep suffering, my own two little boys, and finally the other patients waiting to see me, all fought to rise to the top of my consciousness as I held him for a brief eternity.

The final diagnosis of "superficial wounds" was so inadequate for this man's injury. And I had no hope that the analgesics I prescribed would even touch the wounding of his soul.

Finally, at about five o'clock in the morning, as everything was starting to wind down, I picked up the umpteenth chart citing "abdominal pain." I would have enjoyed seeing a good appendicitis or maybe a hot gall bladder. But when I asked the patient, a middle-aged obese woman, what brought her to the ER, she seemed to think that I'd asked to hear her life story.

"It all started when I was a child, when I got food poisoning..."

I tried to recall my medical school instructor, who admonished us to "let the patients tell their stories. They will give you the diagnosis if you let them." But all I could think was, *Why am I here when I could be home with my wife in a warm bed?* Seeing that this was the last chart in a big stack I decided to let this patient say her piece. Initially I took a few notes, but as her history started to wander, I set the chart on the bedside stand. *I can remember anything important,* I told myself. I took a seat on a stool and pretended to listen intently. Before long, I succumbed to the temptation to rest both elbows on the bed rail while cradling my chin in my hands. I don't know how long it took, but my elbows slowly started sliding apart. Finally I was jolted awake when my chin hit the cold bed rail. I found myself in a strange room with an unknown woman talking about her bowel movements. Drool was running from the corner of my mouth.

"Really," I said when she finally came to a stopping point. "And how do you feel now?" I was praying that we wouldn't have to start all over.

"Actually I feel better now," she said. "You have such a good bedside manner. A real listener."

"Thank you," I said while casually wiping the drool from my face. "I feel better too."

"What was wrong with that lady?" the charge nurse asked as I placed the chart in the Discharge rack. "You were in there forever."

"Uh...food poisoning," I said authoritatively, looking at the one word I had written on the chart. "Has my relief arrived yet?"

2

Bat Bite on Butt

THAT'S WHAT THE CHART SAID, right there under chief complaint. Nothing more. It had to be a joke the nurses were playing on me. They had done that before. They once sent me into a room with a chart that said: "cold." The patient didn't have a cold. The patient was cold and dead. The patient had been sent in to be pronounced with a funeral home. So this had to be a joke.

But when I got to the room, I found a very frightened, embarrassed woman in a bathrobe. On the far end of the gurney was something bloody in a towel. When I asked her what happened, she pointed a very shaky finger at the towel and said: "It bit me!" When I opened it to examine the contents, it took me more than a moment to recognize the beast. The fur and face made it look like a rat. But sure enough, the shattered wings confirmed that it was indeed a bat.

"Where did it bite you?" I asked.

"Right there," she said, as she lifted her hip and pointed right to her rectum.

"OK," I said slowly. "How did this happen?" I was fully expecting to hear one of those kinky urban legends that had passed around every ED about some local celebrity. Everyone who tells one of those stories claims that it happened to someone else, but they know it to be honest to God fact. Swear on a stack of bibles.

"I was in bed and it bit me on the butt," she explained.

Over the years I have developed a technique for eliciting more information without having to ask embarrassing, plain-as-the-nose-on-your-face, obvious, but seemingly nonsensical, questions. It looks like a cross between a math teacher's stare over the glasses and the moment before you belch. I call it "the look." Most of the time you don't even have to add the obvious question, like: "Was there some reason you didn't turn off the garbage disposal before you reached in to get the fork out?" You know, questions like that.

Unfortunately, I had not mastered "the look" at that point in my career and I was forced to ask the obvious.

"How did a bat get into your bed?" And then: "How did the bat get into your underwear?" Not that it mattered to my treatment plan. By now, I was just plain curious.

"Well, you see, my bedroom has huge windows with no screens or curtains," she began. "And since I like to sleep naked, I never turn on the lights. I just leave the covers turned down so I can jump into bed and cover up. When I came to bed after my bath, I just must have jumped right onto the bat. I immediately began screaming, jumped out of bed, turned on the light, grabbed my softball bat and began swinging for all I was worth. The neighbors got a real show and I demolished my room as well as the bat."

After examining the puncture wounds, I explained that the bat was probably healthy and only bit her because she jumped on its head. Nevertheless, the remains of the hapless bat will be sent to the Health Department. She was relieved when I told her that we would begin immunization for rabies without waiting for the results.

By the time she left, she was calm and ready to try bed again. But I couldn't help but wonder if her neighbors ever got the courage to ask if she thought she was Babe Ruth playing midnight naked baseball.

3

An Easy Decision

"**B**ABY WON'T STOP CRYING," was the chief complaint. How many times have I seen that in the past few decades? I never know what to expect. It could be a baby with simple nasal congestion. After all, babies are obligate nose breathers. If their nasal passages are blocked, they can't breathe...unless they're crying. But it could also be an infant with a life-threatening intussusception, where the bowel telescopes within itself. A lot of things swirl through my mind as I traverse the ten yards from the chart rack to the room.

Oh, she was crying all right. The nurse who had placed the mother and child in the room had closed the door in an unsuccessful attempt to dampen the sound. When I opened the door it was like I had stepped onto a factory floor where everyone has to shout at each other over the high-pitched whine of a hundred machines. This little girl was making herself known.

"Whoa, wow!" I said instinctively as the blast hit my ears. "What's the problem, sweetheart?" I cooed to the baby, attempting to assume a soothing voice while reaching out to the mother. The heavyset young mother was clearly at her wits end. She nearly shoved the baby into my arms.

"She's been screaming like this for hours," she shouted over the racket. But then it was like someone pulled the plug on all the machines at once. The child's mouth slammed shut and the room went silent. She immediately began attempting to touch my moustache with her tiny finger. I checked each little finger to see if she had twisted a hair around one of them like a tourniquet, a not infrequent finding. The mother sat dumbfounded. "Really," she said apologetically. "She really has been screaming like that for hours. What did you do?"

"I dunno," I said, shrugging my shoulders. "Are you sick, sweetheart?" I was looking into her piercing blue eyes as she busied herself exploring my face. She had chubby pink cheeks that perfectly matched her pink knit cap. "Or are you just trying to drive your mamma crazy?" Sick or Not Sick; that is the question. It sounds so easy. And sometimes it is. But every time you get comfortable, beware.

Without thinking, I began slowly bouncing in a waltz step while holding the baby. As I began my history, two conversations were going on simultaneously. One, on the outside, was my timeworn litany of questions to the mother. They seemed to roll off without conscious thought. "How long has this been going on? When was her last wet diaper? Has she been around any sick children?" And so on.

On the inside was a cacophony of voices, some urging me to get on with the night's 'more important cases,' some warning me to look for the telltale signs of impending disaster, some just telling me to enjoy the break from the drunks and drug seekers. One of the voices, though, coming from the remote past, offered a bittersweet warning...

• • •

"He'll be fine," I had told my wife after hearing her worry about our own four-month-old.

"I think he is coming down with croup," she said.

"Every kid in town has croup tonight," I said with a hint of exhausted irritation. I had glanced at him when I got home. He did look fine. But I could see her eyes pleading for attention. As I had just finished a long shift in the ER at the local pediatric hospital, I was feeling too exhausted to consider the possibility of another sick kid. I realize now that what I knew then was just enough to be dangerous. A little voice in my head was arrogantly saying, *You're the doctor. What does she know?*

"Put him in here by me," I said, finding a compromise. "I'll watch him while you get a little rest." I absentmindedly took him from her arms and plopped down on the couch to watch some playoff football. "Go on, go to bed. I know you're tired. I'll get you up if I need you." It sounded considerate, but really I just wanted her to quit staring at me so I could watch football.

She finally left the room. I became engrossed in the game, ignoring my infant son's quiet, grunting respirations.

"How's he doing?" my wife asked, coming back into the room after less than a half-hour. She stood in front of the TV vying for my attention.

"I thought you were going to bed," I said, trying to look around her at the screen.

"I thought you were going to watch him," my wife insisted, taking the baby from my arms. "I think he's sick." I could hear genuine anxiety rising in her voice as she shoved our little boy in my face.

Only then did I notice the slight gray cast to his skin, indicating the falling oxygenation of his blood. I also noticed that, to my increasing panic, his respiratory rate was slowing down, not from relaxation but from fatigue. A few more minutes of this and he was going to stop breathing. It took my breath away.

"I think we need to go back to the hospital," I said slowly to my wife, trying to appear calm. It was as if I was speaking to someone who had just stepped on a landmine but had not yet triggered an explosion.

The drive to the hospital was quiet except for our baby's soft crowing.

As was to be expected, he had improved some by the time we arrived. Being exposed to the cool air of the night had reduced the swelling in his airway just enough to avert a disaster. Tom, a fellow classmate in my emergency medicine training program, was still on duty in the ER. Seeing that my son had improved, I suddenly felt apologetic for bringing him to the hospital. "I'm telling you," I said to my friend. "He looked pretty sick."

"Gray, huh?" Tom said with a shrug. "I guess we have to get an ABG."

"Do we have to?" I felt the pain of what he was about to inflict on my son.

"What's he going to do?" my wife asked.

"He needs to draw blood from the baby's artery to check the oxygenation." It was the first time I had experienced the consequences of my words. Many times before I had questioned the observations of patients and demanded a blood test to prove or disprove what they had reported. I, like the parents I had previously discounted, now wanted to bypass the evaluation of the workup and get right to the therapy. "You can see that the pulse ox is low," I said, trying to negotiate with my colleague.

"He's cold and that may be closing down his peripheral circulation," he countered. "He may not be as sick as he looks. Besides, wouldn't you order a gas on some other kid if their parent said he had turned gray?"

Despite the fact that he was holding out a false hope, I knew Tom was right to do this one by the book.

"Let's go for a walk," I told my wife as I pulled her out of the room. "Let's allow them to do their work." My wife still swears that she could hear our little boy's cries from the other end of the hospital.

"He was hypoxic and acidotic," Tom said when we got back. "We got cultures and did an LP just in case he was septic. I didn't wait to get a signed consent from you. I assumed it was OK to proceed." Our son was already surrounded by nurses who were starting an IV in his arm. My heart sank with the possibility that he could indeed be much sicker than I expected. My wife looked at me, cocking her head, as if asking me to translate what my colleague had said.

"His blood oxygen was low. And his pH was too," I said to my wife as tears welled up in her eyes. "He's a sick little guy. There could also be infection so they drew blood cultures and did a spinal tap, just in case."

"He'll need to go to the PICU, just in case we need to tube him," Tom reported.

"Try not to if you can," I began to plead. But before he could return a reasoned response I stopped him. "Just do what you have to do." I didn't need to interpret the intensive care acronym or the intubation reference. She had heard me talk about other babies facing life and death situations and understood the gravity of the situation.

I spent the next week working in the Peds ER by day and sleeping in the PICU waiting room at night. In an effort to hold off intubation the intensivist had placed him in a respiratory tent containing oxygen and helium. The heliox mixture was meant to decrease the airway resistance in his lungs. It was sort of like a lubricant to his scratchy swollen bronchi. But it made his crying sound more like a duck than a baby. Each time I went in to see him he would reach out for me and cry. His tiny chest would collapse almost to his spine as he attempted to breathe on his own. But when I just touched his tiny hand he would smile...and then return to quacking.

• • •

"Do you have children?" the mother asked after all my questions had ceased. Her query broke the magic spell of my little dance partner and me.

"Yes," I smiled suppressing the urge to pull out pictures of children and grandchildren. I finished the exam looking for petechiae between the toes, checking for nuchal rigidity several times, and any other signs of severe infection or other potential catastrophes. I covered every base twice before handing her back to her mother. She immediately started to fuss again.

"That's frustrating," I said. "I thought we had her. Let's try feeding her and see how she does. I don't hear you telling me anything that raises red flags. The vital signs are fine and the physical exam doesn't show me anything. Let me see how she does and then we'll decide whether we need to do a workup." This little one didn't meet any of the standard measures for a sepsis workup, but I wouldn't have hesitated to do it if I thought it necessary. I do not like the idea of doing shotgun tests when you don't know what you're looking for, but I had to show the mother that I was trying. Despite all this, there was just something inside of me that said this little girl was not sick.

Several times I popped back into the room to observe the infant. I realized that I had done nothing except dance around the room with her and talk to her mother. The baby was a little calmer, still fussing and grumping but now only having brief periods of screaming. Was she sick or not? Sometimes I really wished I'd gone into orthopedic surgery. All they have to do is look at the x-ray. Either it's broken or it isn't.

Finally, it was time to fish or cut bait. The baby was back to screaming and the mother was looking exasperated. I walked back into the room and picked up the baby again. This time her screaming continued unabated. The voices lobbying for 'sick' were also getting louder in my head. "I guess we'll need to check some things on your daughter," I shouted over the roar as I danced about the room wildly patting her diapered bottom. The old magic just wasn't working for me this time.

All of a sudden there was an explosive squirting sound that came from her diaper. It sounded like I had jumped on twenty ketchup packages. I peeked into her diaper and found a huge stinky mess. "Whoa, little girl, did that come out of you?" I said to the cutie in my arms. She stopped screaming, looked up at me with a look of dreamy satisfaction, and fell sound asleep.

"Was that all it was?" I asked myself aloud. I looked at her for a long moment. Now she appeared perfectly normal. I looked at the mom who was smiling. *I hope she doesn't think I'm going to change* that *diaper,* I thought, quickly shoveling the baby back into her mother's arms.

The mom just shook her head disapprovingly. I had seen the same look from my wife many years before. "You need a diaper or some wet wipes?" I asked, beating a hasty retreat to the door.

4

What Goes Around

EVERY EMERGENCY DEPARTMENT HAS their frequent flyers, but in a small town the ED staff can get to know some patients like they are members of their own family. Take Ralph, for instance. Everyone knew him. He lived with his aged mother. He was schizophrenic and she was senile. He had more than enough imagination to make up for her forgetfulness. It seemed that in this case two people with half a brain could do quite nicely if they shared. Both received small disability checks so, with the help of neighbors, they were able to get along.

Being more mobile than his mother, Ralph spent his days picking up cans and bottles and redeeming them for the deposits. Frequently (and I do mean frequently), he would show up in the ED with minor complaints. A Band-Aid for a cut, or two Tylenol for some minor pain. The nurses would give him a sandwich and he would be on his way, good as new. Sometimes the problems were real, but many were imaginary. The mental health system was aware of his condition and felt that as long as he was getting along they did not need to intrude into his delusions. The system seemed to work.

On this particular night Ralph was complaining of an earache. He had no fever, no sore throat. I looked at his ear; it appeared normal. I checked his hearing; it seemed OK. Being the new guy in town and unfamiliar with Ralph, I started to embark on a detailed workup of headache of unknown etiology. The nurses were more than a little peeved at the fact that I was rocking a boat that seemed to be getting along nicely.

"You need to go back and talk to Ralph again," the charge nurse said with a chiding voice. I was seated at the nurses' station writing his orders and Ralph's room was at the far end of the ED.

"He thinks he knows what's wrong with his ear," she said. I had a lot of patients to see and didn't have time for any silliness. I had a brief staring contest with the charge, which she quickly won.

"OK," I said with a sigh, grabbing my pile of charts and heading for the back.

"I know what's bothering my ear, Doc," Ralph said.

"Really," I responded with a frustrated exhalation.

"Yeah," he said with his voice trailing off. "They put a radio tower by my house to listen to my thoughts." In almost a whisper he added, "and it's boring a hole in my ear."

"Oh," I said, looking down at the CT scan order on his chart. "Maybe you don't really need this."

Satisfied that at least his problem was not medical, I sat down and attempted to explain away his delusion. He would have none of it. He claimed he was in great pain. I don't like to deal with problems this way but I thought I would try a placebo. I didn't want to give him a real analgesic and possibly cover up a real problem. So I ordered some antacid and told him it would help his condition. It was miraculous; he said the pain was gone completely. He told me I was the best doctor he had ever had, and that he would come back whenever he had a tough problem like this one.

As he was leaving he walked by the charge nurse and me, thanking all the staff for their wonderful care. His huge gut and slight hips made his pants droop exposing half his buttocks. I couldn't help commenting to the nurse about his clothing. He was wearing a sweatshirt from a major university and the ugliest pants I had ever seen. They were a bold plaid of hot pink and lime green. They were filthy from what was obviously daily wear.

"Have you ever seen such ugly pants before?" I mused absentmindedly to the nurse. "He looks like a clown."

"Yes," she said with a roll of her eyes. "He wears them every time he comes to the ER, which is often. And," she added as she started to walk away, "they belonged to my husband."

"Ralph stole your husband's pants?" I asked, chasing her down the hall.

"No," she stopped. "Those were his favorite golf pants. But I hated them so much I sneaked them out of the house and gave them to the Goodwill. I told my husband that the cleaners lost them. Ralph must have gotten them at the Goodwill. Now I see them ten times more than ever."

"Did you give Ralph a sandwich?" I said, baiting her.

"No," she shot back. "Then he'd come back even sooner."

5

Take a Deep Breath

FROM TIME TO TIME I'VE BEEN asked about my most embarrassing moment in the ED. While there have been more than a few, I guess this would rank right up there near the top. From a physiological standpoint, I think this is what happens when you concentrate too hard and disengage the speech centers of your brain. At least that's my excuse.

The patient was a matronly fifty-year-old lady. To describe her as "stout" was an understatement. I'm sure she had raised a house full of linebackers. It was the low cortisol hours of the morning by the time I got to her. And she was about the fiftieth patient I had seen that night, so I was really tired. Nevertheless, I entered the room and introduced myself with my utmost professionalism. Despite my attempts at clinical formality, it was clear that the setting made her uncomfortable as she sat primly on the bed in her starched hospital gown. Her complaint of chest pain was rather nondescript and seemed at first glance unlikely to be cardiac in etiology. But she was quite worried and I took her concerns seriously.

After taking a thorough cardiac history I was even more convinced that her heart was not the source of her pain. But I knew I would have to explain my thinking to convince her. She had no risk factors for heart disease. Though of stocky build, she was not truly obese. She had no diabetes and had never smoked. She hadn't even been around smokers. Despite her build she was not hypertensive, explained by the fact that she lived on three floors and climbed the stairs incessantly all day long. Without even a trace of leg swelling, she denied any shortness of breath whatsoever. But she did complain of a bronchial cough over the last week to ten days. The pain was sharply localized over her left anterior chest wall. And it was made worse by taking a deep breath. I suspected pleurisy and hoped to hear a pleural friction rub if I listened closely to her chest.

Finishing the history, I launched into the physical exam, all the while talking to her about the possible causes of chest pain. While peering through the ophthalmoscope at her eyes I explained that without any risk factors she was an unlikely candidate to get cardiac chest pain at rest. While shining a flashlight down her throat and examining her lymph nodes for enlargement, I commented on the paucity of findings there as well, explaining that even a case of pneumonia seemed unlikely with these findings.

When I got to the lung exam I was talking, thinking, and examining at the same time while she sat rigidly on the bed. "I don't think you have much to worry about," I assured her as I warmed the stethoscope with my breath to ease the shock of cold metal on the back. Placing the bell of the stethoscope on her back, I closed my eyes to concentrate on the subtle distinctions of wheeze, rales, crackles, and rubs. Slowly I moved the stethoscope over her back noting the dullness of her diaphragmatic margins, the absence of egophony, or the presence of adventitious sounds. When I'm in that space I'm like an audiophile listening for the oboe entrance in one of Bach's concertos. I was in my own little clinical world. Between each instruction to breathe deeply, hold your breath, say "E", I would explain what I heard, or didn't hear, like a tour guide at the philharmonic. My exam was coming to a clinical diagnostic crescendo as I zeroed in on the left anterior chest wall where I expected to find the pathology. I began coaching her to take deep respirations to maximize the chance of hearing the rub; that unique sound, like one rocking in a saddle that is made by an inflamed pleural lining rubbing an equally irritated internal chest wall. "Take a deep breath," I said slowly as I inched over her chest looking for that special spot. "Big breath," I commanded as I moved closer to the money shot. "B...i...i...i...g br...e....a...t...h."

Finally I reached the spot of maximal pain on inspiration where I was sure I would find what I had long suspected, a pleural friction rub. *Eureka!* "I have the diagnosis," I reassured her.

"Oh really," I heard her muffled voice through the stethoscope. "What is it?"

I wanted to confirm what I had heard so I commanded her to take one more deep breath before I explained. "B...i...i...g b...r...e...a...th. Yes," I said rather exultantly, "you have...you have............B...i....i...g" just then I opened my eyes to explain my findings, "Breast!" I was standing there, proud of my diagnostic acumen, staring at her ample bosom.

The silence was deafening. But inside my head I was screaming *BREATH! Breath, you ninny!! Big breath!* She pulled up her gown while looking at me like I was a Peeping Tom. I thought for a nanosecond about explaining the neurological link between the visual and speech centers in the brain. But mostly I just wondered how I could anatomically get my foot out of my oral cavity. In reality, my mouth went dry and my voice closed up completely. I think I mumbled something about pleurisy and heart pain while looking at the chart, the bed, and finally my shoe laces. I never looked up but I could feel the dumbfounded expression on her face. As I left the room I explained to the nurse that the patient could have anything she needed for pain. "Anything!"

"All she's got is a few little pains," she said. "Oh," I said ominously. "They're a lot bigger than you think."

6

My Mona Lisa

I CAN STILL SEE HER SITTING THERE with an expression of boredom. She was a young nineteen-year-old, with creamy skin and long dark hair. And her eyes. Eyes that watched my every movement as I worked. But those eyes had already seen too much in her few years. The police told me that she was married to a man who was in jail for beating her with a tire iron. Their only reason for bringing her to the ED was that she was behaving strangely outside a convenience store. She had bought a little over a dollar's worth of gas. She wasn't talking to herself or anything. She just seemed "confused."

In any event, when she got to the ED she had decided, it seemed, that she was not going to talk to me or cooperate in any way. To every question, she just gave a bland smile.

"What's your name?" I asked warmly as if meeting a new friend, even though I knew her name from the police report.

"I don't know," was her reply, with a look of boredom. Her speech was clear, responsive, and organized—just negative.

"Where do you live?" I asked with a curious smile. Her only reply was a shrug and a brief search of my eyes.

"Do you know where you are?" Another look of boredom and a flip of the hair.

"I don't know."

"Do you really not know or would you rather not talk? It's OK if you don't want to talk right now. I can come back later. Would you like a cup of coffee or a glass of juice?"

A look of irritation. "I don't know."

"Well, it's obvious that you don't want to talk. Maybe I can come back in a moment. Are you sure you wouldn't like something?"

Now she totally ignored me.

I spoke with the police again. They seemed vaguely familiar with her. One officer thought she came from a good family but had gotten off-track somewhere. Was she homeless? They weren't sure. They thought she was staying at the Salvation Army. It was close by. Had she done anything that was threatening in any way? No. It was just that she seemed lost. And when they tried to help, all she would say was: "I don't know." Now she was mine.

I went back to try to entice her with small talk. Still no answers. So I broke out the velvet hammer.

"I'm really sorry," I explained. "But since you were brought here by the police it is my responsibility to make sure you are OK. Until you talk to me I can't let you go home, wherever that is. Just make yourself comfortable here. I'll have the staff give you some food if you like. Just let me know when you are ready to talk."

She seemed to understand and gave no resistance to my plan. Her nurse placed her in a chair outside her room and put a sandwich and a glass or orange juice in front of her. For over four hours she sat placidly with an enigmatic smile watching me work. I felt like I was trying to warm up a cautious infant. I would catch her looking at me and wave. I even spoke to her without looking directly at her and she would answer. Her thoughts seemed organized. Reality testing seemed OK. There didn't seem any obvious fear or paranoia. But if I tried to go any deeper, she would look away coldly. Then if I returned to my charting, I would see her, from the corner of my eye, intensely studying my face.

As the morning approached I became concerned that I was either going to have to turn her over to the day shift with the only complaint of not wanting to talk to me, or discharging her—to where, the street?

I finally broke through when I asked her if she was under arrest or if there were any outstanding warrants for her. She suddenly began speaking normally and said that she didn't need to be in the ED. She knew who she was, where she was, and there was nothing wrong with her. *Alright,* I thought. *We're finally getting somewhere.* But as soon as I asked anything more personal, she reverted to her standard: "I don't know."

"We found her grandmother," a deputy sheriff said, approaching me at the nurses' station.

"What did she have to say about her?"

"She's not saying much more than this gal," he said with a shrug. It was obvious he had the same shift pressures that I had and was just happy to be able to punt this one. "She said she's had a hard life."

"But is there any mental illness? Suicide? Anything?" I wanted to put something in the medical record. He just shrugged.

"I'm going to call your grandmother and she is going to come get you. Is that OK?" I was looking for anything that would indicate she felt unsafe in her environment. Nothing. At least nothing in the eyes that I recognized.

When morning came, I asked if she would like to go home. She nodded her head slowly. I had no reason to keep her. She had no real complaints. And I was starting to get busy again. I told the nurses that when her grandmother arrived I was to be called so I could get to the bottom of the story. But a code arrived and I disappeared for over an hour. When I came out she was gone.

"They waited for a while," the charge explained. "But we couldn't keep them any longer. They just left."

"Oh well," I was resigned to chalk this one off as a strange, yet beautiful, enigma. I assumed I would never see her again.

Two days later, she hung herself behind the convenience store where she had attempted to buy a dollar's worth of gas. When I heard the news, I was overwhelmed with feelings of failure and despair. Had she said something that I missed? Was her flippancy really psychosis? Would deeper investigation have revealed the desperate situation in which she perceived herself? Would somebody else have picked up a red flag that signaled her need for help? The whole department was in shock. All questions, no answers.

Sometimes when I have worked a long string of nights, in my exhaustion I will wake up in the middle of the day and be disoriented. Today was one of those days. I was jolted awake by a strange sound. But when I tried to clear my senses to orient myself, the room was dark and I could only see a tiny bit of daylight through the slits in the drapes. For a moment, I wasn't sure where I was or what was happening. All I could see was her face with that quizzical look: "I don't know."

7

Slap of Life

THE RADIO CRACKLED THAT A SINGLE patrolman would be bringing in a gunshot wound to the chest just as the squad car screeched to a halt in the ambulance bay. In this city, the police had learned that waiting for an EMS unit with an angry crowd can be a dicey proposition. So they just throw them in the back seat and get the heck out of Dodge.

Even though I ran to the ambulance doors I barely beat one of our new nurses. "He been shot in the chest," the out-of-breath cop blurted.

Sure enough, as soon as I threw open the door, I saw a limp teen with a bullet hole dead center in the front of his leather jacket. I dead lifted him onto the stretcher and the nurse climbed onto the gurney on top of him to start CPR while shouting instructions to the other staff to prepare for chest tubes and a possible open thoracotomy. I had learned to crack chests at the Baltimore Shock Trauma unit. But I had never done it so many times as here in this city.

We raced down the hall as people appeared from other rooms. The respiratory therapist who had been giving an asthma treatment to a nearby patient had already begun setting up the laryngoscope and endotracheal tubes for intubation of the patient's airway. I could hear the oxygen hissing and the bag and mask were ready, hanging on the wall. A nurse began preparing the auto infuser that would take blood from the chest, filter it, and re-infuse it back into the patient. Another nurse opened up two chest tube trays with trocars that looked like great big nails. Once the skin incisions were made in the lateral chest wall, these trocars could be plunged deep into the chest cavity, allowing the chest tubes to be attached to suction. Other nurses were hanging IV setups and warming the blood we kept handy in the trauma bay. An orderly was even breaking out a Foley catheter to insert in the patient's penis. And finally, the charge nurse was opening the tray that contained the rib spreaders in case I needed to make an incision from sternum to axilla to gain direct access to the heart and lungs. We had done this many times before and the team worked like a well-oiled machine.

I'm kind of a big guy and the patient was a slightly built teen, so I didn't bother to ask for help from anyone to transfer the patient from the gurney to the trauma table. That's when I noticed that something just wasn't right about this kid.

He wasn't limp enough. I know that sounds strange. But people who are dead or nearly dead are really limp. And this kid wasn't. So as the nurses were cutting off his pants to gain access to his groin for our biggest femoral IVs, I just leaned over and shouted in his face while gently slapping his cheeks: "Hey, kid. What happened!?"

I know it seemed like a really dumb question. He had a bullet in his chest, right? But hey, it's no dumber than when we come upon a patient who has collapsed in the street from a cardiac arrest and we reflexively shout, "Annie, Annie are you OK?"

Well, of course, this patient made no answer. Just an eyelid flutter. Without thinking about it I gave him a really hard slap on the face, just like Rhett Butler slapped Scarlet O'Hara in *Gone with the Wind*. To which he jumped up and screamed: "I've been shot!"

Just then a small caliber bullet fell out of his underwear. Everyone just stopped and took a big breath without exhaling. I looked at the hole in his leather jacket. It was right where the thickest layers of leather were overlapping. When I unsnapped his coat I found only a tiny bruise on his chest wall. Not one drop of blood. Everyone was suddenly deflated.

Someone shouted sarcastically: "Cancel the trauma code!" The Blood Bank tech came running in and saw everyone breaking down. That usually meant that the patient was dead with no possibility of resuscitation. But the patient was sitting up wearing only a leather jacket, cutaway underpants, and a dumb look. Some just stopped what they were doing and went back to their coffee. The nurse that had been riding the patient down the hallway doing chest compressions attempted to sneak out of the room without being seen. But I am always one to snatch victory out of the jaws of defeat.

"Do you realize what I've just done?" I announced to the crowd. "I've just discovered the next lifesaving technique. I'm going to call it the Plaster Slap of Life. If Valsalva can have his maneuver and Heimlich his thrust, I can have the Slap of Life." It seemed to catch everyone's interest, lightening the mood in the room while we milled about, completely ignoring the patient.

"Can you describe the maneuver in biomechanical terms?" queried the trauma resident. He was always the one looking for a new paper to publish.

"Yes, I can," I said authoritatively. "The operator's weight is forward on the balls of the feet with the non-dominant foot slightly forward. The hand is raised to plane of the operator's chest. The elbow is flexed to a 105 degree angle. The fingers are held tightly to make a firm even striking surface. The arm is swung through a 180 degree arc with the fingers striking the victim's cheeks between the malar eminence and the mandible. (The hand is gloved with a latex-free glove, of course. Universal precautions must be observed while not exposing the victim to a potential latex allergy reaction.)"

"I think this needs a little refinement," the resident added. "But if I help you modify this for the patient in the C-collar, it should be called the Plaster/Martin Slap of Life."

"Now if we start doing that, we're going to end up like WPW or LGL, with something like P/M SOL. I can barely remember Wolf-Parkinson-White. Who ever remembers Long, or Ganong, or worse, Levine," I counseled. "No, I recommend that you start the certification courses for PSOL, the Plaster Slap Of Life. Maybe you could let the medicine guys do PSOL and you could do TPSOL for trauma cases. See? I'm already doing it."

"I guess you're right," he conceded. "Besides, people should be re-certified every year for such a difficult maneuver. We could run the courses for three or four hundred dollars a head. Who cares about fame if we have fortune?"

I was beginning to think that I had given away the farm for an obscure reference in a dusty textbook. "Maybe I could start the American Board of SOL." Now that really was ridiculous. *You can't have a whole board exam on SOL,* I thought. *But you could have a mega-code SOL practicum, where we practiced slapping each other.* As I started to walk back to the nurses' station I began thinking, I could start the *National Registry of Slap of Life. That could keep me lecturing for the rest of my career.*

"Hey! What about me?" I heard a voice from behind me in the trauma room.

"Oh, how's your chest?" I asked.

"It's pretty sore, but it's my jaw that really hurts."

"Oh, that's from being SOLed," I explained.

"SOL?" he asked.

"Yeah," I mumbled, "you won't understand. That's a medical term."

8

A Legend in His Own Mind

IT WAS BITTER COLD OUTSIDE. And I suspected that the little man in the last cubicle was just trying to find a warm place to spend the night until I looked at the chart and saw that he had a fever. So he really was sick. OK. But what did he have? What I saw in the next few minutes changed my life forever.

Your first impression of a patient can tell you so much. We all know that sometimes you can even make the diagnosis without hearing a word of the history or even touching the patient. So I am acutely aware that I need to pay attention to those inner voices that come to me when I first meet a patient.

The patient was a big man in a little man's body. What I mean is that he seemed to project himself like the executive of a large corporation. But he was really just a little old man in a filthy secondhand three-piece suit. It was clear that he tried to shave regularly. But he obviously hadn't been to the Salvation Army shelter in a few days and he had several days of stubble. His suit, which had once been tailored to someone slightly larger, was frayed and filthy. There was a fine layer of oily soot over every exposed surface—body and clothing. That was a sign that he had spent many nights sleeping on the grates that vented warm polluted air from deep beneath the city. However, a closer look at his clothing showed telltale signs of a deeper problem.

On all the surfaces of prolonged contact with the sidewalk—hips, sides, shoulders and knees—there was the stain of body fluid that evidenced an infected pressure sore beneath it. In my experience, it wasn't uncommon to find alcoholics who, like this patient, would lie for hours in an alcoholic stupor crushing the soft tissues of his body at the points of contact. I suspected that once we removed his clothing, we would find him covered in sores. These patients often developed septicemia from these sores. Moreover, from the sound of his cough, he was likely to have pneumonia. But one thing was clear, he was not going to get better, even with antibiotics, as long as he was continuing to shower his bloodstream with bacteria from his pressure sores. So before talking to him for more than a minute, I began to formulate my plan: remove all the infected clothing, establish the diagnosis by exam and the requisite blood tests and x-rays; clean and debride his wounds; and load him with antibiotics. It was a simple case. In no time he would be well on his way to recovery.

However, there was one obstacle.

When I began to examine the man, I found that he had several layers of clothing, typical for street people in the winter. Moreover, his wounds had been draining for some time. And apparently, when he would soak one layer with exudate from his sores, he would simply cover them over by putting on another layer of clothing. So multiple layers of clothing were firmly adherent to each of his many wounds, forming several filthy, contaminated, coagulated masses. It was clear that soaking the clothing even with peroxide would take hours. The clothing would simply have to be cut away. But the man would have nothing of it. In his eyes, those clothes were the symbols of his status as a human being. He wasn't just another bum on the street. He was an executive that had fallen on some hard times. It wasn't the pain that he feared, but the nakedness.

I had no time to negotiate with his delusional pride. I was determined. The clothes would have to come off. But when I tried to bully him into obeying me, he threatened to leave. We were at a stand off. I could have let him go. But I felt that if his life wasn't already in jeopardy, it would be soon. So I finally resorted to begging him to trust me. He was a man who clearly trusted no one but himself. I told him that he was sick and that these clothes were actually making him sicker.

"How could that be?" he asked, clutching his oversized coat to his chest. "This is an expensive suit. I can't let you just cut it up." But all I saw were rotten rags.

"We have to remove them for you to get well. Trust me," I repeated. "I'll admit that it's going to be painful removing your clothing. But I'll do what I can. And once they are removed you will start to get better."

His body ache of his fever and his cough were starting to get to him. I could tell that his resistance was starting to crumble. "Hey, I've got some other clothes in the back that are clean. After we clean and bandage your wounds I will give you some nicer clothes."

Finally, he relented. Slowly we soaked, cut, and pulled away several layers of clothing to reveal an emaciated, wounded old man. He was clearly humiliated by his nakedness. But he seemed to improve with each stroke of the soapy sponge. When the procedure was finished, he seemed swallowed up in his clean hospital gown. But he was smiling and cautiously grateful. His fever had broken, antibiotics were running, and his wounds were covered with comforting suave. I told him he had to go upstairs for a few days to heal, but that we wouldn't forget about those new clothes when it was his time to leave.

Years later, I recalled this man. He came to me one night, it seemed, out my dreams. At the time, I was at the pinnacle of my career, successful and intensely proud of it. But I was desperately unhappy. My marriage, as a symbol of my life in general, had all the outward trappings of the American dream. But on the inside there was only pain, loneliness, distrust, and reaching for false fulfillment. I was desperately sick.

Then one night when I was lost and alone, crying out for someone to help, I recalled this man. I had become him, intoxicated with myself and high on the legend I'd become in my own mind. But I, too, was really only covering up the wounds that lay beneath. I had to trust someone to begin the process of removing my rags of self-righteousness. I finally understood why he was so afraid. The pain of removing the clothing was nothing compared to the fear of seeing what lay beneath. Revealing our nakedness, our ugliness, to the bright light of examination was healing but also humbling and frightening. The handsome cloak that was once self-respect had become the shroud of conceit and arrogance and had to be removed.

Like him, someone stepped to my aid. It wasn't easy but after it was done, I found it also wasn't as hard as I thought it would be. Even today that patient frequently comes to mind. And I wonder if he remembers and thinks of me as often as I think of the one who rescued me.

9

Innocence Lost

SOME NIGHTS IT SEEMS THAT bad things really do happen in sets of three. The first two were back-to-back, two girls from different worlds afflicted by the same insidious disease.

The first chart's chief complaint was "vaginal bleeding." The patient was fourteen years old and had recently been started on birth control pills ostensibly for the purpose of controlling her menstrual irregularity. She had no other complaints other than the bleeding. No cramping, backache, burning urine, nausea, or anything else. So, on the surface, it seemed like her visit to the ER was just for the reassurance of her overprotective mother. However, the concern for this problem seemed out of proportion for the wee hours of the morning. Obviously, something else was going on here.

I discovered the real problem when I asked her if she was sexually active. It's a routine question that I attempt to ask even the youngest girls without any hint of judgment. I just want the truth. She stared me directly in the eyes with a look of cold indifference.

"Yes," she said flatly.

Her mother's lack of reaction told me that this was not news to her. Now a picture of a different nature was starting to emerge. This suburban mom wanted to know if she had a pregnant teenager. The nurses had done their routine urine pregnancy test, which was, to my relief, negative. The news of this was followed by a long, controlled sigh from the mother as if she had been holding her breath since triage. The girl, however, was unfazed by the news. I couldn't tell from her reaction whether she was not surprised by the report...or just didn't care.

The picture started to come into focus, however, when I explained that I would need to perform the pelvic exam. Even though I told the mom she could stay in the room as a part of my pre-exam explanation of the procedure, she left the room with all the disinterest of a crowd leaving a late inning baseball game that seemed already decided. Then, without one shred of self-consciousness, the teenager stood up, dropped her thong underpants and laid back on the exam table with her legs wide for the exam. I was embarrassed that she wasn't. What had happened to this child's innocence? She had the shaved pubis and relaxed pelvis of a sexual professional. But what was worse, she had the mental detachment that accompanied it—and all at the tender age of fourteen.

After the exam and cultures for STDs I tried to talk to her about safe sex practices. But the bored look told me she had heard it before and was ready to go. Then from my heart I blurted out, "You know, sweetheart, you don't have to have sex to be loved. Tell your boyfriends that if they really love you, they can show you by treating you with respect. You know, you're really worth that."

There was a brief flicker of a smile like a candle that is just about to blow out, then nothing. Without a word she got up, dressed, and left.

The next patient was worse off than the first. An urban twelve-year-old, living with her single mother and her various boyfriends, she complained only of intermittent abdominal pain. It was her mother that got right to the problem.

"I want her tested for pregnancy," she demanded. She had a free-floating anger at the world that just happened to land on me. While the test was being run I asked the girl if she had had sexual intercourse with anyone. The clinical term seemed to confuse her. She just looked at me dumbly.

"Have you had sex?" I asked bluntly.

"Uh huh," she replied, nodding slowly while putting her hand to her mouth.

"How long has this been going on?" I asked. More blank looks.

"You know how many times, girl," the mother said menacingly. "Tell the man how long this has been going on."

Finally her daughter told of having sex with an older teenage boy for the past year. It started when she was eleven.

"Have you known this was going on?" I demanded from the mother. "Don't you realize that this is rape?"

"I don't know anything about it," she shot back. "And besides, he's gone now."

Trying to achieve something positive out of the situation, I tried the same old safe sex discussion that I had just delivered. But my anger at the educational establishment and at the mother and daughter for their naiveté just grew with each answer. Yes, she did know how to put a condom on a banana. But no, her "boyfriend" never used one. I was so frustrated after leaving the room that I reported the incident to child protective services.

"Who is protecting these children from sexual predators?" I wondered aloud to anyone who would hear. Through ignorance or indifference, these mothers seemed powerless to stop the train that was crushing the life and spirit from their daughters. Then I realized something. *Where were their fathers?* Neither of these girls had a dad. I cursed the men who had abandoned their children. But as my anger rose, I started to hear the message in my own ears. I, too, had a fourteen-year-old daughter. *Had I been there when she needed a dad?* I couldn't say. As the night went on I became more and more anxious to get home. I felt like I was helplessly watching a house fire. I couldn't wait to rush home to check on the safety of my own loved ones.

Arriving home before anyone had awakened, I went directly to my daughter's room. At first I just stood at the door and marveled at how much she had grown into a young woman while I wasn't watching. But then I was clutched with guilt for all my absenteeism. Was she to be the third neglected child I would see this morning? Before long I found myself kneeling at her bedside, half praying, half babbling apologies for all the events in her life that I had missed. Even though I was stroking her hand she slept peacefully until I said, "I promise you can say anything to me about boyfriends, dating, sex, anything."

"Oh, Daddy," she yawned. "What are you talking about? I don't have a boyfriend."

"You don't?" I said. *Where had I been?* "What about all those calls and letters? What about the balloons that boy sent?"

"I told him I wasn't ready to have a boyfriend," she said with eyes half closed.

"Oh," I said, surprised, as she fell back asleep.

I kissed her cheek and picked up the book she was reading, *A Christmas Carol*. Suddenly a flood of relief came to my eyes. Slumping to the floor, I sat for a long while in a period of self-reflection, repentance, and prayer. I finally rose with a new resolve. It was time to go to bed. But I knew that Scrooge would awaken from his dreams, and Christmas was not over yet.

10

Tricks and Treats

WHY DO KIDS PUT BEANS UP their noses? Are they just so accustomed to having their fingers in there that it seems the normal thing to do? And it would be one thing if they just put the objects near the opening of the nose, where they can be easily retrieved. But no. Their little fingers always seem to shove them halfway to their occipital lobe. I asked these questions of the last three-year-old who was admitted with a candy bead up his nose. He just looked at me with an irresistibly cute smirk that said, "It sounded like fun to me!" I guess I've done some stupid things myself. He didn't seem to be in any distress. And he was so cute in his clown costume, with his big mop of curly blonde hair, deep blue eyes, and mischievous grin. He had no idea what kind of torture was in store for him getting that darn thing out. I certainly didn't want to spoil his fun, but there was no way around it.

I have used a variety of techniques for grasping a slippery object deep in a wiggly kid's nose. I've tried using bayonet forceps in the past. Even the name of the instrument sounds dangerous. It's like using a pair of chopsticks to retrieve a bowling ball from deep within a manhole. The kid would be screaming. The nose inevitably would start bleeding. I would be standing and sweating, using a combination of a head lamp, binocular magnifying glasses and a nasal speculum just to see the dang thing. Whichever nurse drew the short straw would be doing a WWF wrestling move trying to hang on to the kid while the mother was pressed into the corner with her mouth covered, fire in her eyes, ready to kill me for hurting her precious baby. And the worst part was that if I couldn't get it out, I had to call an ENT guy who would abuse me on the phone for a half an hour before dragging the kid to the OR to spend $20,000 on a three-minute procedure.

In this particular case I didn't think I could reach the object with bayonets and momentarily contemplated punting to ENT from the start. But I knew that the parents were in no mood for waiting.

"What would happen if he sucked it into his lung?" they asked anxiously.

"Oh, he'll cough it out," I said, but my response would not do. There had to be a better way.

My father always said that a job was easy if you had the right tool.

"You know those little tweezer-like forceps that just open at the end?" I asked the nurse. "I've seen the ENT guys use them. Do we have a pair in the ED?"

"Ooh, yes," she said with a wink. "I keep them hidden just for these cases. They always seem to walk away." But fate was just baiting me with an easy solution. "No dice," she said after returning. "Somebody discovered my hiding place."

"Can we get a pair from the OR?" I pleaded.

"You'll have to talk to the nursing supervisor about that," she said with a doubtful shrug.

I tried to explain what I was looking for to the supervisor, but she hadn't done real nursing in twenty years and didn't have a clue as to what I was asking for. She finally brought the entire ENT cart from the OR.

Surely, I thought, *I'll find what I need here*. But still no luck. I know it would have been the perfect instrument.

"What about a suction catheter?" one of the nurses suggested, looking at the pile of instruments. "That should work."

Should have, could have, would have! I was beginning to think that I had a black cloud over my head. Soon, the nurse had the screaming child in a half-nelson wrestling hold, and I had the suction so far up his nose I was afraid that if I touched nasal tissue I would suck out his pituitary. But the bead would not budge.

I was not going to call the ENT. I did not have the stomach for his abuse that night. But I was at a crossroads.

Then I remembered reading in one of those throwaways about a nifty little trick where you give the kid a little puff of mouth to mouth while holding the other nostril closed. "The bead will just pop out," the writer guaranteed. "No trauma. No digging. No bleeding." It sounded like the perfect solution. If it worked, everybody would be happy, most of all me.

After all the trauma we had inflicted on this poor little guy, it seemed to me that the key to success would be a little surprise. So with only the briefest explanation to the mother, I laid the kid down on the table once more. Expecting the worst his mouth flew wide open and he began wailing. But this time, instead of sticking something in his nose I simply grabbed hold of his chin and closed off his opposite nostril with the thumb of my other hand. And just as he let out his first giant wail, I placed my mouth over his and give a big puff.

What came next was good news and bad news. The bead popped out all right. It rolled into my breast pocket. That was good.

The bad news was that his giant exhalation, combined with my giant "puff," caused everything from his upper airway to his nasopharynx to explode through his only open orifice. A giant glob of snot hit me right in the side of the face. I jumped back dripping with mucus. The child and the parents were relieved, and stunned, by the result of the strange procedure. The nurse started to snicker, but controlled a full belly laugh. By the time I finished cleaning up in the bathroom it was obvious she had told the whole staff what happened. They, too, were tight-lipped until I heard one of the old nurses mumble, "Way to take one for the team, doc."

Next time I'd try a little harder to get those special forceps.

11

Image Is Everything, Almost

I HAVE ALWAYS FELT THAT THE IMAGE of a physician is important. I don't mean the image of someone who lives in a big house, drives an expensive car, and plays golf every Wednesday (although there is something to be said for the therapeutic power of luxury). I don't know anyone who, when they are planning to have some difficult surgery, looks in the phone book for an ad that says "Cheaper, but just as good." No sir! If the procedure is really expensive, it must be the best.

Rather, I'm thinking about the personal image of the physician. I've worn my share of slouchy clothes and worn-out sneakers, but I've also come to realize that patients have more confidence in a physician that, well, looks like a physician. We can't all look like Marcus Welby, MD (does anybody even remember him?). But it does seem that patients have more confidence in physicians that have a certain air of knowledge and command of the situation. These physicians' patients do what they are told, some with incredible accuracy and detail. (Like the guy who was told not to lift anything until his hernia was fixed...he refused to do anything around the house for two years until his wife drove him off.) These physicians are asked fewer dumb questions. This can be a real asset.

I once knew a guy who wore a surgical hat, shoe covers, and a mask around his neck at all times—although he never went to surgery and seldom used the mask. Part of it was that he was a surgeon wannabe. But another part of it was that he had discovered that his patients treated him like he knew something. We all thought he was silly to try looking like a brain surgeon while examining sore throats, but his patients hung on his every word. While I still wouldn't wear shoe covers, I did learn to do as many things as possible to instill confidence in my diagnosis and treatment.

For instance, I'd wear a starched white coat over my scrubs and be rather formal in my introduction. With a name like mine, if I even cracked a smile during the introduction the patients might think I was joking. Before any procedure that's frightening or painful, I'd look the patient squarely in the eyes and sternly say that if they do exactly as I tell them everything will go well. I must confess that I've even stooped to peering over my glasses in the attempt to browbeat a patient into feeling confidence in me. It usually worked, but sometimes I was my own worst enemy. Like this one night...

The patient was a middle-aged woman. She was just at the wrong place at the wrong time as she walked through her husband's garage workshop while he was grinding a metal engine part. A gentle puff of the fan and she suddenly had a metal shaving in her eye. Her eye was watering furiously and she was scared to even open it. Finally, after commanding her in my sternest voice to relax and remove her hands from her face, I was able to see the small black dot buried in the center of her cornea that was the source of all her discomfort. I calmly lowered the lights in the room and told her I was going to put some drops in her eye to ease the pain. However, each time I tried to drop the anesthetic she would squeeze her eyes shut. When I eventually succeeded in instilling the drops, she howled at the initial burning sensation. But after that had subsided she was relieved to find that the pain was finally gone. Her confidence in me soared. I explained that I would use a big microscope, called a slit lamp, to remove the metal from her eye. I reassured her that she would not feel a thing. And since her eye would be so close to my hand, she would actually see nothing that I was doing. She seemed pleased that the procedure would be quick and easy, and readily allowed me to position her head in the brace that held the slit lamp at the proper distance. Almost without her knowing, I used the tip of a needle to lift the metal fragment from her cornea surface. With each painless step my professional stature seemed to grow in her eyes. But now came the hard part.

I explained that the metal had left a rust ring that needed to be removed using a tiny buffing tool. I only explained it that way because our corneal burr made a high-pitched sound that unnerved many people because it reminded them of a dentist's drill. Again, I explained that she would neither feel it nor see me do it, just as long as she remained still for me to do a good job. But as soon as the drilling noise began she jerked her head out of the brace.

"I don't know about this," she started. "Have you ever done this before?" she asked, swallowing hard.

I have to admit that it was a little unnerving for me to have her yank her head out of the microscope while I was a millimeter away from her eye with a spinning drill.

"I'll need your full cooperation," I admonished in my deepest professional baritone, "and yes, I've done this hundreds of times."

Then, in one of my best moves, I leaned my chin on my thumb and forefinger, peered over my glasses, calmly put my other hand on her shoulder and said, "You'll do fine. Just trust me."

That did it. Sort of. She relaxed, but not completely. She was on the plane, she trusted the pilot, but she was still going to grip the seat.

I repositioned her in the chair with her chin in the slit lamp brace. I adjusted the light, the lens, and had her look at the exact spot to position the rust ring in the middle of the slit lamp's visual field. As I started to lower the corneal burr to her eye I realized that her seat was slightly too low. This caused her head to drift back and the rust ring to come out of focus. To correct the situation all I had to do was touch the foot pedal and bring her chair up a few inches. But I found that the pedal was slightly out of the reach of my foot. I felt that if I just stretched a bit further, I could adjust her position without having to reset the patient. However, just as my right leg reached its maximum stretch, my weight shifted suddenly and the stool on which I was seated shot out from under me. I fell to the floor with a loud crash as my head landed in the rolling trash basin. This time my patient really jerked her head out of the brace.

Everything I had done to instill confidence was lost. I looked up into her eyes and saw sheer terror. She had finally gotten herself onto the airplane and Bozo the clown had revealed himself to be the pilot. I tried to make a lame complaint about the seat but it was no use. To her credit she still allowed me to remove the rust ring. It actually went smoothly. But I could hear the grinding of her dentures as I performed the procedure.

Sometimes this image thing is overrated. Sometimes it's just better to be quick.

12

Triage

GOOD EMERGENCY PHYSICIANS MUST HAVE a strong trait for multitasking in tense situations. Residency training attempts to hone those personality traits and nascent skills. And the final oral exam of the American Board of Emergency Medicine attempts to test that ability by having the examinee face a board of examiners, all asking questions simultaneously about different kinds of cases. Some examiners even inject emotion into the already tense experience. I always performed well under those circumstances, but nothing could have prepared me for the test that awaited me one night in Trauma Rooms 1 and 2.

Having worked as hard and fast as I could for the first seven hours of my shift, I felt I was due a short break. The ER was temporarily empty. So I retired to the call room to put up my feet. I have to admit, I was a little irritated when I immediately got a call that a ninety-year-old was arriving in a few minutes in full cardiac arrest. I didn't mind handling the code, even if it was probably a useless effort. But it seemed like the nurses could have alerted me before I got comfortable in the call room.

"Doctor to Trauma 1," I heard the clerk shout over the intercom a second time, as I sauntered down the short hallway.

"I heard you!" I said, raising my voice.

When I entered the room containing the beds designated Trauma 1 and its adjoining Trauma 2, I did not, however, encounter a ninety-year-old, but rather two infants, nine- and three-months-old, both in cardiac arrest. The two cases appeared totally unrelated. It was like getting hit by lightening twice, simultaneously.

The nursing staff had already started chest compressions with basic mouth-to-mouth on one child. This little boy's mother stood at the foot of his bed silencing a scream with a hand over her mouth while jumping up and down like she had just hit her thumb with a hammer. The second child, who had arrived within a minute of the first, lay in the next bed with virtually no one around. Her mother was standing there, jaw set, seemingly trying with all her effort to stop her shaking. The only nurse in that room was frantically trying to get cardiac monitor leads on the patient's tiny chest. Both sides of the room, separated by a thin curtain, were studies in contrast and similarity. The side of the room with all the nurses exploded with shouts directing the initial resuscitation and the released screams of the mother. The other side was stricken and silent.

For what seemed like an eternity, I stood at the door surveying the two worlds. We didn't have enough staff to run two simultaneous pediatric codes. I heard the intercom calling throughout the hospital for assistance. But this was a small facility and I knew that I was the only doctor in the house.

I went to the quiet side of the room first. The patient wasn't breathing, but she had a pulse. Weak and slow, but at least she had one. It was a one-man code while the nurse tried to find what I needed. I stuck my head around the curtain and saw that the monitor only displayed compressions. The looks on the nurses' faces told me what I already suspected. I finally got a bag and started puffing the infant. I needed more help, but I couldn't pull staff away from the other baby. The awful truth of the situation started to sink in. To save this infant I needed everyone's full attention immediately. The truth was that we had one infant we could save and one that we couldn't.

The mother in Trauma 1 screamed even louder, wilting to the floor. When I would peer around the curtain, her imploring eyes were almost more than I could take. She finally cried out, "Why aren't you doing something for my baby?"

I succumbed to the pressure when a respiratory tech arrived and took over the assisted breathing of the baby girl. Against my better judgment I took the time to start an intraosseous line and push cardiac meds. But nothing was working. Meanwhile, I kept hearing "I have a weak pulse over here" from the nurse on the other side of the curtain. CPR, intubation, drugs, shock, nothing was working. It was clear that nothing was going to work. This was a SIDS. But leaving the child's bedside was abandoning all hope for his mother.

Finally, I summoned the courage to do what I had needed to do sooner. Without making eye contact with the mother I told the respiratory therapist and the nurse's aide to continue doing CPR but the rest of the staff needed to come work on the other child. By the time we got back to the baby in Trauma 2 her pulse and pulse ox had dropped. Whether it was due to poor technique by the nurse or not, I was cursing myself for delaying. I immediately intubated the infant and saw a rise in her pulse oximetery. After a quick IO line, a bolus of fluid and a little glucose, her pulse started to quicken. There was a lot more to do, but we would win this one.

There is nothing like the exhilaration of a pediatric rescue. But that night it was tempered by the cloud of pain that hung over the ER. Putting my arm around her, I quietly reassured the mother of Trauma 2, not wanting to be overheard in Trauma 1. She melted into quiet tears, relaxing for the first time, and tried to hold on to me. But I broke away, steeling myself for what I needed to do, and stepped to the other side of the room to take one last look at the monitor.

"Hold CPR," I said mechanically. The monitor was completely flat. There was no cardiac or respiratory motion whatsoever. "Zero two thirty-four," I told the therapist quietly for the record. It was the official time of death—the end of this child's brief life. I knelt down to face the mother who sat sobbing on the floor. I reached for her hand. The other was still clutched at her face. When our eyes finally met I just shook my head.

"I'm sorry," I said. "I'm so sorry."

When the shift was finally over I was completely spent. The rest of the night had been slow, but I was exhausted. I just slumped in my car before leaving for home, numbly reviewing the experience. *Did I do everything I could have? Did I give up too soon?* I was too tired to even think. It would have to do.

Years later, I sat for my emergency medicine recertification oral exam. It's a test that has to be taken every ten years. I was given the option of a written or oral exam. I thought the oral exam sounded easier and truer to the experience of a practicing physician. I recall the final set of examiners giving me the facts of the last three test cases. The first two were straightforward, but the third was a pediatric cardiac arrest. I calmly went through the algorithm of treatment options for each, with success for two of the three. But the peds case failed to respond to every therapy I tried. I was expecting at least one of them to result in a save, but nothing worked. I thought I must have forgotten something. I went over my actions again and again, yet found nothing wrong. I fought back panic. I studied the face of the examiner for any clue of an omission. He was poker-faced.

Finally I said, "This baby is dead."

"Is there anything else you would like to say? Is there anything else that you would do?"

I paused for one last review of my answer. "I would console the mother."

"Thank you, Dr. Plaster. This concludes the exam," he said without expression.

In the hotel bar, where everyone congregated after taking the exam, this case was discussed ad nauseam. Many had done more than I, some going through the algorithm several times. But we all ended with the same result.

Later in the day I shared an elevator with the same examiner. "That was a hell of a case you gave me."

"Yeah," he said with a look of exhaustion. "Just try seeing that case all day long."

"Did I do OK?" I pleaded after a moment of respectful silence. I was hoping he would break his oath of confidentiality and give me a sign.

"Yeah," he said with a look of an experienced colleague. "You did OK."

13

Friendly Fire

YOU'D THINK THAT AFTER FOUR YEARS of college, four years of medical school, and three years of specialty training, people (and I mean the people you work with) would treat you like you know something, right? Well, not always. There is often someone who second-guesses everything you do. It doesn't come as an outright challenge to your judgment, it's just, "Are you sure about [fill-in-the-blank]?" Sometimes you feel like asking, "Uh, and which medical school did you graduate from?"

That's not to say that you need to listen to every naysayer. That would drive you crazy. But one of the best pieces of advice I ever received was from an old doctor who used to give grand rounds to us as interns. He would listen to us pontificate about various topics. Then he would say, "Just as important as knowing what you know, you need to know what you don't know." At the time, I had no idea of what he meant. But thirty years later, and after more than a few near misses, I think I'm starting to catch on.

Unless they have been there, no one quite understands the pressure to make quick judgments in the ED. On any given night a busy emergency physician might see thirty to forty patients with a variety of complaints. That doesn't sound like much if you do the math: fifteen to twenty minutes per patient. That should be enough, right? And some nights they can be all minor or straightforward problems that even the person of modest medical intelligence can diagnose and treat safely. But some nights even the simple problems wave little red flags that require extra scrutiny. And the pressure to keep moving can obscure your vision and judgment. That's when a challenge to your judgment can be so maddening... and so necessary.

When I arrived at 7:00 p.m. to start my twelve-hour shift, I noticed that the to-see rack was overflowing and the post-triage rack was double stacked. That meant that every room was filled with a patient who was yet to be seen and there were many more waiting for those rooms as I emptied them out. The doctor who left me this mess ran for the door as if she never wanted to see another emergency department.

"Can you call another doctor?" a patient implored as I rushed into the room with a stack of charts.

"I wish I could," was all I would say. The fact was that the emergency department was simply understaffed for the number of patients that came to the ED. No one was at fault; there simply were not enough doctors qualified and willing to do the job. And it was a waste of precious time to explain to every patient that the hospital had actually flown me in from out of state to help deal with the crisis. It was better for me to simply see the patients as efficiently as possible—"move the meat" as ERs docs say irreverently behind closed doors. Then I picked up Ken's chart.

Ken was complaining of localized chest wall pain. Actually he wasn't complaining at all. His wife had made him come to the ED after she heard him complaining and rubbing his chest at home. He was a robust man with close-cropped hair and the handshake of a construction worker. He had very few real risk factors for cardiac pain. He had smoked years before and had only the mildest of hypertension. But his pain didn't radiate nor was it associated with any other symptoms. Moreover, he described his pain as sharply localized and limited to the chest wall, the usual history for pleurisy. Except for this seemingly minor complaint, he was a picture of health.

A nurse had gotten a routine EKG that demonstrated a left bundle branch block. While abnormal, this finding in itself was not particularly alarming. His pain was largely gone by the time I saw him, except for some localized tenderness to palpation. All in all, I was thoroughly underwhelmed with the story for angina. He had another story though, one that fascinated me. When asked if he had ever had surgery, he blandly told me he had been shot in the chest once. His clean-cut appearance didn't fit the profile of the all the gangbangers with gunshot wounds that I was accustomed to treating. Seeing my quizzical look, he added: "Vietnam." But then he became silent and there was a distant sadness in his face.

"How did it happen?" I asked. Somehow I sensed that this story had never been told. He seemed like the kind of man's man who would only share this burden with another man of the Vietnam era.

"Friendly fire," he said, shaking his head in remembrance. "I was just a kid. But I told the Sarge that I had seen a truck off-loading some of our guys in the same area where we were working. I can still remember his look. 'When I want you to do recon, Lance Corporal, I'll tell you,'" Ken said, mocking the sergeant's voice. "'There are no friendlies out here. Not possible!' It wasn't thirty minutes later when I heard the pop of a grenade launcher just like mine. Next thing I knew, all hell broke loose. I swam across a creek with my thumb blown off and a hole in my chest, hoping I could hide under a bridge. When the firing stopped, we had killed three of them and they had killed two of our guys. Only thing was, we were all marines." He seemed exhausted after sharing the story. "I told him," he mumbled flatly, "the Sarge just didn't listen."

It had happened over thirty years before, but the pain was still with him. After a long pause, I felt that attention to the present, whatever his problem, was a healthy relief from the pain of the past. I outlined the routine chest pain work-up. I explained that I doubted we would find anything more serious than sore muscles. He was fine with that and wanted to get home as soon as possible.

Well, you know how it goes. If you want the lab to be quick, they behave like stubborn children, passive-aggressively thwarting any attempts at speed. First, the blood was labeled improperly. Then it was hemolyzed and had to be redrawn. This went on for several hours. Ken felt fine and was frustrated with waiting. He wanted to go home, and I needed his room to see more patients.

"I think I'm going to let this guy go home," I said to a nurse who seemed to have a special talent for annoying me. "We'll call him if anything is abnormal."

"Are you sure about that?" Miss Spectacles chimed in. "His wife said he was in a lot of pain at home. He sure sounded like angina to me."

I hated it when she said things like that. *He's been in that bed for three-plus hours without turning a hair,* I thought. *Enough was enough. I think I know angina when I see it. Besides, I'm the doctor here. You're just the nurse.*

Of course, while thinking that, I just gave a fake smile and ground my teeth. There would be no hope of clearing up this mess any time tonight. I would still be looking at the same logjam when I stumbled out of this place at eight o'clock tomorrow morning. And I would have Miss Spectacles to thank for making a bad night even worse.

Ken was really getting irritated with me by the time his second set of cardiac enzymes came back. To my surprise, they were borderline positive. Not positive, mind you; just high enough to make me look at him with a different eye. Now I was thinking that just maybe he did have something going on. He trusted my judgment so it was easy to talk him into staying overnight. "It's just a precaution," I told him. I still didn't think he would rule in.

But he did. While in the ICU that night, he had more pain and ended up going to the cath lab. The cardiologist, reluctant as I was at first, actually found a high-grade lesion in his left main coronary artery. A simple stent corrected what could have been a catastrophe had he been discharged. The cardiologist said that I probably saved his life.

Before the end of my shift Ken's wife came by the ED to thank me. When she left, I turned to Miss Spectacles and said, "Thanks for your input on that case."

She said nothing, just glanced at me over her glasses. I hated it when she did that.

14

Science and Art

I'VE ALWAYS HAD THE RULE that if a child *looks* like they need a spinal tap to rule out meningitis, they do. Even if everything else seems normal. Don't ask me what that means. I don't know. You'd think that a doctor is all about science. And certainly as a night shift wears on, I lean more heavily on the statistics of a situation to make a decision. But I'm always aware of falling into cookbook medicine. Sometimes you just have to go with a hunch. For one thing, all the clinical decision rules, the algorithms by which we decide what to do, have some element of subjectivity to them. And our 'objective' data sometimes reflects more of what is going on inside of us than we realize. A lab result may fall outside the normal range, but only a bit. Is it lab error or simple variance? Is it the beginning of something that will have a catastrophic ending? You either see what you fear most or deny what you see when it doesn't fit the picture in your head. So the decision that comes out depends on the data that goes in. GIGO, as the computer geeks say it, garbage in/garbage out. So while I always take into consideration the objective data, in the final analysis, I don't let it drive the decision. It seems to me that there is another dimension to decision making that transcends good vs. bad data. Some decisions require a hunch, or an intuition, if you like. It's like a voice inside that speaks in inaudible tones. You ignore it at your peril. I learned that concept a long time ago.

The ED was absolutely packed with children from a flu epidemic. I thanked God that I was working an ED with double physician coverage plus a PA until the wee hours of the morning or I would have drowned in the patient load. All together we had seen, it seemed, a hundred children that evening with the same symptoms of fever, lethargy, headache, mild vomiting, mild cough, and varying degrees of dehydration. A few were getting IVs, but most could be treated with oral hydration, antipyretics, rest, and close observation. It was before we had any antivirals, but as we now know, those drugs have very little effect on outcome anyway.

After seeing about thirty kids that looked alike, I came into the room of a five-year-old boy and his mother. He was well nourished, well developed, and well dressed. His mother seemed a bit overprotective. She struck me as a rich professional woman with an only child. In retrospect I realize that she wasn't very excited about trusting her child to a young doctor who may or may not know what he's talking about. In any event, my first impression of this child was that he was sicker than the others. And I told her so. He was hot and lethargic. But then again, so were all the other sick kids. His neck wasn't stiff, but it wasn't particularly relaxed either. Of course his fever made him ache all over, I told myself. So any movement was going to draw some complaint and resistance. Nevertheless, I told her that I was going to draw some blood samples and then do a lumbar puncture.

"What's that?" she asked.

"You know, a spinal tap," I explained. I couldn't tell whether she didn't like the idea of someone putting a needle in her kid's back or just the idea of me doing it.

"Have you done that before?" she asked, examining my youthful face. I both understood and resented her challenge of my judgment. She didn't know it, but I had a young child too. I wouldn't want some young, inexperienced doctor sticking a needle in my son's spine. But I was experienced at the procedure and asking my partner to stay even later because the patient didn't trust my skill was just too much.

I know what I'm doing, I thought, *and it has to be done.*

"Of course," I reassured her. "I've done this hundreds of times." I hated it when I lied like that. And it was clear that she wasn't reassured by my obvious self-aggrandizement. In fact, I realized then that I had no margin for error. Getting a sick child to curl up in a ball and inserting a four-inch needle into his back to hit a half-inch space three inches deep can be a challenge. I could see from this mother's face that I would have only one chance.

Then it all started to come apart. While the lab tech was coming to draw the blood, the Tylenol that the child had received in triage started to kick in and his fever came down. With that he looked and felt better. Not great, but definitely a lot better. He sat up and drank some Gatorade. He even smiled at his mother. When his blood count results came back, they were completely normal. Well, not exactly. His white count was a little low, consistent with a viral infection. So when I went back in to talk with the mother about his results, she asked the obvious question, "Are you sure he needs to have the spinal tap?"

She had touched the point of my vulnerability. Did I trust my own judgment? It was obvious that she didn't want me to do the tap. Maybe it wasn't really necessary.

"OK," I sighed uneasily. "I think I'll pass on the LP. We can just treat his fever and watch him closely at home. If anything changes you can bring him back." I quietly slid the lumbar puncture informed consent sheet under the take-home instructions. As I began filling out the instruction sheet detailing what signs and symptoms the mom should look for, I couldn't escape the fact that he had come in with these same problems. In the middle of writing my note I just absentmindedly got up, walked out of the room, and began wandering the ER, pondering what course to take. As my colleague was walking past the nurses' station on his way out the door, I asked one final time what he would do.

"If you thought about it," he said, "there was a reason. Have a good night." And he happily, quickly made his way out the ambulance doors.

Sheepishly, I reentered the room.

"We really need to do the tap," I explained. Amazingly, and to her credit, she agreed. I guess she really did trust me. But I wasn't even sure I trusted myself. I was still shaking my head as we wrestled him into position and started the procedure. I had a feeling I was doing the right thing, but I hated the thought of taking a kid who already felt bad and torturing him with a needless procedure. I was still berating myself as the needle popped through the dura to drain the spinal fluid. What I saw then stopped my breath: the CSF looked like frank pus. He was mere hours away from developing full-blown meningitis, sepsis, and sure death.

The science of medicine kicked back in as high dose antibiotics and a brief stay in the ICU made this a memorable, though somewhat straightforward case. He lived, of course, and was discharged a few days later with nothing more than a good story to tell his grandchildren.

But I wondered, *what had stopped me from discharging the child?* Why couldn't I send that kid home? Was someone standing beside me, holding me back? Or was it just pure random choice? Was the voice warning me not to send this child home within me? Or was it the voice of past training, or some other internal voice? I wondered, *am I just a mechanic tinkering with a very complex machine, or am I an artist who can somehow see and release the life and beauty from a block of stone?*

I was still wondering at this mystery as I entered the room of my last case that night, a chubby baby girl.

"She doesn't seem right," the mother stated vaguely. "I don't know what's wrong with her." I listened to the mother's story. But as I gazed intently at the little girl I realized that I was listening to the child tell her own story. It was nothing but babble, but I was beginning to believe that I could hear something more.

15

Discomfort Zones

EVERYONE HAS THEM, EVEN DOCTORS—things that we are called on to do every day, yet we never quite get over feeling a bit squeamish about them. They might be situations or procedures that, even though you've done them a thousand times, you avoid as often as you can. As hard as you try to be comfortable with the situation, you just aren't. For me, and I'm embarrassed to say this, it's rectal exams.

They say that if you are bitten by a dog as a child, you will be afraid of dogs all of your life. Well, let's just say I was bitten by this "dog" in med school.

When I went through school we didn't have "professional patients" like some schools have today, actors who are paid to come in and let med students poke and prod them. Our instructors were old-school and thought we needed to personally experience some of the finer aspects of the physical exam before we inflicted our ignorance on patients. Since we were already paired off into lab partners for our cadaver dissections, we didn't have to draw lots to see who we'd be torturing.

We drew blood from each other's veins, started IVs, and passed nasogastric tubes to test stomach acid. Drawing blood wasn't too hard. Mike, my partner, was a huge guy with veins like water mains. He had been the Kansas state wrestling champion in his weight division. So, even though I'd never done anything like it before, my attempt to draw blood was successful on the first try. And he returned the favor. IVs were a little more anxiety producing. First, they involved bigger needles. And second, we had to use the back of the hand instead of the larger veins located in the crook of the elbow, soon to be known as the antecubital fossa. Nevertheless, Mike started my IV without a hitch. But when I attempted to follow suit, I ran into some problems. Despite his huge hands, his juicy veins seem to dodge and roll. It was like trying to stab spaghetti with a fork. I can still recall how his face reddened and his muscles strained as I painstakingly inched through his tough skin, probing for a vein.

Next came the nasogastric tubes. The thought of a plastic tube being jammed in my nose and going down my throat, gagging me as it went, was bad enough. But having Mike do it to me made my blood run cold. I knew he was bent on revenge, so I volunteered to pass my own. Each time the tube touched the back of my throat it caused me to retch like a drunken sailor. Mike would offer to "help" me.

"No thank you!" I echoed into the trashcan over which I was kneeling.

Just when I thought we were finished torturing each other, the instructor announced that the following week we'd be doing rectal exams. I couldn't help but notice the devilish grin that came across my lab partner's face as he popped the knuckles on his huge hands. My anal sphincter tightened.

"What's it like getting a rectal exam?" I asked Marty, a classmate of mine in the year ahead.

"It felt like his finger was going to touch my tonsil," he said, squinting his eyes like he was telling a ghost story to some Cub Scouts. "When he took his finger out I shot shit all over the wall. It was horrible."

My jaw went slack. The pale look on my face let him know that I had swallowed the bait hook, line, and sinker.

Marty continued by telling me about a guy who took an exam glove and filled it with water. After tying off the wrist and shaping it in the form of a fist with the index finger extended, he froze it hard as a rock. With his lab partner in position, the prankster sneaked the frozen hand out from beneath the table, lubed up the finger and...

"What happened?" I gasped, feeling a chill run through my body.

"The guy leaped off the table and ran out of the room with his pants down around his ankles. The rest of the class was in the waiting room."

"What happened then?" I rasped.

"I think he either left school, killed himself, or went into psychiatry. I'm not sure."

That was enough for me. I was sick the day the instructor taught the practical on rectal exams. I think I had leukemia or a broken leg or something else terrible. I just know I wasn't anywhere near the clinics.

When we actually started clinical rotations, one of my first experiences was with a gastroenterologist. He didn't do digital rectal exams. He went for the full monty doing sigmoidoscopy. And he didn't use a flexible sigmoidoscope like we have today; instead, he preferred a stainless steel scope, which he lovingly referred to as the "silver stallion." With a light at the end of the rigid scope, it allowed direct visualization of the rectosigmoid bowel through a tiny glass door. The insufflator port on the side, attached to a small bulb, allowed the examiner to pump air into the colon, expanding so as to see even better. But if he ever opened the door to do a biopsy, he would quickly dodge any material that might come out with the whoosh of air. The hapless medical student looking over his shoulder was like an umpire set up behind a catcher. If he failed to react quickly enough, he'd likely get hit by a "foul tip." I barely saw more than the back of the doctor's head during the entire month.

Consequently, I was totally unprepared to examine that part of the human anatomy once it became my turn to be the real doctor.

One of my first rotations was the ER. And as luck would have it, one of my first patients to require a rectal exam was a rather attractive woman in her thirties. "Have you ever had a rectal exam?" I asked, hoping she would refuse.

"Of course," she responded. "Every time I get a pelvic."

"Have they ever tested you for passing blood?" I followed, hoping someone else had done it for me.

"I don't know," she said.

I was trapped. I thought of lying about the result, but I knew I'd get caught by my professor. Finally, I placed her on her side, like the booked illustrated. But when I went to actually perform the examination something went terribly wrong. I must have turned my head, or closed my eyes, or something. I felt no hemorrhoids, or stool, or... *Oh no, that's the cervix, you idiot! How could you miss the rectum?*

"Is that a new way to do a rectal exam?" she asked trustingly over her shoulder.

"Uh, yes," I said. "If there are any hemorrhoids I don't want to start them bleeding." I was shocked at how quickly this whopper of a lie jumped out of my red face. I left the room as quickly as I could, telling the unit clerk to schedule the patient for sigmoidoscopy next month when I would conveniently be on cardiology.

Although I eventually got to where I could do the exam, I continued to avoid it at all cost. But one time I picked up the chart of a young man and, to my chagrin, his complaint was that of rectal bleeding. After trying every way I could to rationalize my way out of it, I reluctantly told him that I had to give him a rectal exam.

"You have to do what??" he almost shouted.

"I have to put my finger in your bottom to see what the problem is," I sighed. We looked at each other like condemned men.

"That sounds nasty," he said, contorting his face.

"I'll have a rubber glove on," I said incredulously.

"Will it hurt?"

Then I told him the doctor's traditional lie. "It'll be a little uncomfortable."

When I had finally coached him into the knee chest position on the exam table, the rectal sphincter just would not relax. The harder I pushed, the tighter he became and the further up the exam table he crawled. I felt like I was pushing a car with my fingertip. With his head mashed against the wall, I finally got the tip of my finger through the orifice. But it was a worthless exam. His sphincter was so tight that it cut off the blood from the tip of my finger. I could barely feel anything.

After the exam he virtually leaped off the table muttering to himself. *I'd make a lousy proctologist, I thought.*

I must admit that my fear of rectal exams has always been a good reason not to go to one of my colleagues for routine testing. But my wife finally put her foot down.

"It's time you had a thorough physical exam," she demanded. Adding insult to injury, my wife, who is younger, taunted me saying: "And you know what this means, don't you? After fifty you need regular checks of your prostate and colon. Do you want me to make the appointment?"

"Don't worry honey, I'll make the call." I first had to check to make sure my old lab partner was practicing in another state.

16

Terror

SOME YEARS AGO, NO ONE THOUGHT about locking the doors to the ER. For crying out loud, this was an ER and people need to get in. Besides, this was a small town, Americana. People didn't even lock the doors to their homes at night. We didn't need identification at the bank to cash a check. We trusted newcomers. We were safe. At least that's what we thought.

It was a busy night, like always. We were the only major ER in a rural region between two metropolitan areas. The local town sported a tiny but crowded ski area that kept the ED hopping in the winter, and an interstate that kept it busy in the summer. In fact, the hospital had just built a new and expanded ED. However, the plan was so spread out that the whole loop from one end of the ED to the other was a twentieth of a mile. The trauma and cardiac resuscitation rooms were located immediately to the left of the ambulance doors that opened automatically when the crews approached with a patient. The remainder of the ED was spread out in a series of loops and halls, out of sight of the main nurses' station.

Andrew, the emergency physician on duty, had just seen a cardiac patient whom he thought was stable before hurrying off to the back rooms with an arm full of charts. So he never saw the odd character that came through the self-opening ambulance doors. In fact, no one really noticed him even though he was in full view of the nurses' station. This was a small town where most of the ambulances were operated by volunteer fire companies. Most of the volunteers were salt-of-the-earth farm folks, but there were still a few odd ducks among the bunch. So even though he looked a little strange, no one gave him a second thought...until he reached the nurses' station.

When he got to the closed curtain across the front of the cardiac room he seemed to startle at the noises from within. From his position in the wide hall he could see the legs of nurses moving about behind the curtain. Silently he made a pivot to his left to face the curtain. When he did, Cathy, the only RN standing behind the chest-high counter of the nurses' station, caught a glint of something in his right hand. He was carrying a six-inch butcher knife. Admitting to the ludicrous nature of her courtesy afterwards, Cathy said the first thing that came to her mind at the time: "May I help you sir?"

Without making a sound the man turned away from the cardiac curtains to face her. It was then that she finally, really saw him. He was a total stranger, but he looked at her with the cold eyes of one who had harbored hate for ages. Having treated many psychiatrically unstable patients, Cathy tried to remain professional, even smiling. But any thoughts of dissuading this man's twisted intentions quickly fled as he made his first step toward the counter. Trying desperately to keep control of the situation, Cathy turned to the unit clerk, who, seated before her computer, was unaware of anything that was happening.

"Call security, please," she choked.

"What?" questioned the clerk. The hospital "security force," like many others, was neither secure nor did they carry force. They were kindly, unarmed retirees that helped patients to and from the parking lot.

"Call security!" Cathy demanded, revealing the full measure of her terror. But it was too late.

Before the clerk could even pick up the phone, the assailant dove over the counter. Cathy's first sensation was that her left upper chest had been struck very hard by a fist. Then there was a second blow as the assailant crashed over the counter falling to the floor. The surprised unit clerk was the first to scream. The second scream came from Cathy as she saw the knife buried in her chest. Without thinking she pulled out the knife, spurting blood all over the counter and the assailant who was now lying quietly on the floor. Having spent his fury, he lay sobbing.

"I'm sorry, I'm sorry," he wailed.

The nurses in the cardiac room threw open the curtains to find Cathy drenched in blood. More screaming ensued. Cathy spun and stumbled to the trauma room with the nurses doing their best to help her along the way.

Andrew, having heard the screaming, came running back to the nurses' station only to find everyone but the unit clerk gone. He thought something had gone terribly wrong in the cardiac room, but the cardiac patient was fine. Meanwhile the clerk was screaming unintelligibly at something behind the counter that was obscured from his view. Then he heard the commotion in the trauma room and ran there to find Cathy on the trauma table covered in blood. Nurses were trying to start IVs in her arms as the life seemed to be draining out of her body. But their hands were shaking so badly and their eyes so blurred by tears that it was almost impossible.

"Cathy's been stabbed," they all seemed to scream in unison. Andrew exploded in a long string of expletives that vented all his feelings of anger, fear, frustration, and utter helplessness. Then he set to work.

"Get her clothes off. Get a good IV. Put her on a monitor, O2, and pulse oximeter. And set up the chest tube tray," he finally said. Sticking his head out of the trauma room he shouted, "Call the police, get security, and page thoracic surgery."

As each successive group appeared there were more shouted expletives before settling down to work. The local police arrived in minutes and quickly cuffed the sobbing assailant before dragging him out the ambulance doors to their squad car.

The chest tube got placed with the help of a shaky thoracic surgeon. After several units of blood, Cathy was whisked off to radiology to see if any major vessels had been penetrated.

For a while everyone just stood around crying and consoling one another. Others came from home to help, but everyone stayed their entire shift because there were still patients to be seen. Some of them were very ill.

They got a new ambulance door after that, the kind that required a code to get in. And the security guards were allowed to carry Mace. But the most amazing thing that happened after that incident was that everyone came back to work the next day.

Following that episode, life became very unstable for all of us. We didn't feel like the world was safe any more. Watching the news one night as the commentators discussed America's preparedness for chemical, nuclear, or biological war, my wife asked me "What are we supposed to do if we have a terrorist attack? Should I get some duct tape and stock up on water, Cipro, and Potassium?" She was acting like a mom.

"That's not a bad idea," I responded. Realizing the seriousness of her questions, I put down my reading. "If a terrorist explodes a dirty bomb it will shower radioactive dust. If you're out, go home immediately. Take off your clothing in the garage. Shower thoroughly. Then tape up the doors and windows. Take your potassium iodide and wait for the all clear." I could see her making a mental list. If anything happened I could see her doing exactly as I had described...and surviving.

"But what will we do then?" she said. The fierceness in her eyes spoke of the will to live, but also the dread of the loss of innocence that such an event would herald.

"Terror is only terror if..."

"If it has the power to incapacitate you, I know," she interrupted. I was being pedantic because, loving to discuss politics, we had had this discussion many times before, only in the abstract. Squinting her eyes and setting her jaw, she said, "We do what we've always done. We go back to work and live our lives."

"That's right," I said. "We go back to work."

17

Sick Day

"DOES IT FEEL COLD IN HERE to you?" I called to my wife as I got out of bed and stumbled, shivering, to the shower. It had been a longer string of nights than usual and I was not looking forward to another shift.

"It feels fine to me," she called back. "Are you getting a fever?" I've never known how to take comments like that. I've only practiced medicine for a zillion years. One would think that I'd know when I'm sick.

"Oh, you do feel feverish," she said after putting her hand to my head. I stood there in my pajamas like a kindergartner hoping not to have to go to school. "I think you're getting the flu," she said conclusively. I wish I could do that with my patients. Just feel their head. Look sympathetic. And then announce the diagnosis.

"I think you better stay home."

I stared at her, shaking my head.

"Don't look at me like I've two heads. Just call in sick! You've never done that."

"Exactly," I said, with a sigh of exasperation. "I've never done that... because I can't do that!"

"I know you have sick days. How many years have you worked at that hospital?" she demanded.

"I've got plenty of sick days," I explained. "But it does me no good if there isn't anybody to fill in for me."

It was no use arguing with her. But I knew the answer already. It was three in the afternoon and the chance of finding someone to fill in a night shift at the last minute was slim to none. But to appease my wife, I made the calls. Everyone I could reach was sympathetic, but they all had obligations, had other shifts, or a million other reasons why they couldn't help. Finally, I convinced my wife that I was headed to work.

"This is dumb. You're going to get everyone who comes to the hospital sicker," she said as I bundled up to walk to the car.

"No good deed ever goes unpunished," I mumbled to myself. "You'd think she would praise me for doing my duty even when I don't feel well. But Nooo! I'm the big dummy for going to work sick." I was still muttering to myself as I came through the ambulance entrance doors. I stopped in my tracks when I saw the patient board.

"Oh, no," I said out loud. Dr. Stanford had worked the day shift and he was as slow as a fungus. The board was full, the halls were full, and I could see a stack of charts of patients waiting for rooms.

"You better have your skates on tonight," Helen, the charge nurse, announced as she whizzed by.

"Give me six Ibuprofens and a big cup of black coffee," I said to the Stacy, our newest nurse. She still treated me with some respect. I knew the others would only give me that "Do I look like your slave?" look.

"Isn't your ulcer deep enough yet, doc?" Sonya said sarcastically.

"Hey, where's all the love, guys?" I looked around. "I thought this was like 'the caring professions.'" They all stopped and looked at me. I slinked into the break room just as Stacy was coming out with the coffee.

"We've had Dr. Standstill all day. So we're a little backed up," she said apologetically.

"That's what you guys call Marv behind his back?" I said, slightly irritated.

"Oh, ...oh, ...no! I don't!" she sputtered. "Just some of the old nurses. Well, I don't mean 'old'. Oh, you know what I mean."

"Yeah, yeah, I do know what you mean," I finally muttered, walking away. "Nobody cuts anybody any slack around here." I donned a surgical mask and headed to the first case.

"He must have just come from surgery," I heard a middle-aged lady whisper to her husband.

"You're going to scare the kids with that mask." It was Helen again. I just scowled under my mask. But she was right. The first patient was a little three-year-old girl who recoiled into her mother's arms at the first sight of me. I just slumped onto the examining stool.

"Britney's got an ear infection again and needs some Amoxil. That always seems to work for her. And you don't look like you feel so well yourself," the mom said, reaching out to put a hand on my forehead. I began to obediently write a script for Amoxil.

"I think I'm getting a little cold," I mumbled under the mask.

"I've got some Echinacea that will help," she said as she started to go through her purse.

"That's OK," I said as I closed the chart and started for the door. I stopped myself and attempted to do a physical exam. But Britney was too scared and wiggly for me really see anything. I finally finished my halfhearted exam and left. After several more patients stared uneasily at the 'man with the mask' I decided to at least have a little fun while I felt crummy. So I drew a big nose and mouth with a tooth missing on my mask. Some of the little patients loved it.

"You're such a goofball," Helen said, shaking her head as I came back to the nurses' station. I'd actually gotten used to the mask and forgotten that

I looked silly. "If an administrator comes by here and sees you wearing that silly mask, you're going to get a letter."

"Have you ever seen an administrator on this shift?" I returned. "Besides, the little guys love it."

She just shook her head in mock disgust. I trudged on through the night slowly clearing the To-See rack, then Triage, then Waiting Room. By 5:00am the small piece of gray morning sky that could be seen through the ambulance doors was starting to turn a little pink. I was on my last legs and dreaming about sitting down in the call room as I picked up the last chart.

"What's with the mask?" said the jovial little man in the electrical union jacket. His bald head, short, stocky build, and rough hands spoke of years of hard work. But before I could answer he went on, "I've just had this pain in my jaw off and on all night. I told my wife it was just my teeth. So doc, how about looking at my teeth and giving me some Motrin so I can go to work." I desperately wanted to make quick work of this, but a voice of warning came drifting through the fog of fatigue sounding like a bell on a shoal. I asked a few more questions. They were all negative. But still the bell sounded.

"It probably is your teeth," I finally said, "but humor me on this one and let's get an EKG." You know the drill. The STs were equivocal. The patient got even more impatient as I insisted on enzyme studies. But they were weakly positive. So I called the cardiologist and convinced him to come in early and put him on the front end of the cath schedule.

My long sought-after rest never happened.

"Well did he have anything major wrong?" my wife asked, after hearing the recitation of the night's cases. I just stared numbly at my bowl of oatmeal.

"Yeah," I mumbled, "he had a 95 percent lesion of his left main. He was sitting on a time bomb."

"So you saved his life!" my wife said, with a touch of the layman's awe for medicine. "That's amazing. I guess it was good that you went to work."

"Yeah, I guess it was," I admitted with resignation. "Can I go to bed now?"

18

Betrayal

EMERGENCY PHYSICIANS ARE WELL KNOWN, sometimes even legendary, for their ability to spot a fake. I once walked into a room where the patient was having a violent "seizure." The patient was thrashing and foaming. The bed was rocking wildly. And the nurses were scrambling around the room getting airways, oxygen, IVs, and valium. Spotting the real problem right away, I walked calmly to the patient's side, grabbed her face and shouted "Stop this right now!" She immediately stopped her pseudo-seizure and began talking normally. From then on the nurses treated me as if I could walk on water. But sometimes even the shrewdest clinician can be fooled, if he lets his heart get involved. That's when it stings the worst.

It was late, the ER was busy, but I was just getting revved up. I breezed into one exam room to find a slightly chubby, middle-aged woman, sitting in a wheel chair with her foot elevated. She was plainly dressed with home-permed hair. She reminded me of my mother. Her twentysomething daughter was sitting and calmly conversing with her as I entered the room. I had picked up her triaged x-ray on the way into the room. It was normal. Trying not to inflict needless pain, I examined her ankle gingerly. The ligaments were stable. She reacted very little to my exam in fact. *She's probably delivered five babies in her life. An injury like this is nothing to her,* I thought. It seemed to be a garden variety ankle sprain. The ankle was definitely large, but absorbed with being sympathetic, I never bothered to compare the size of the injured ankle to its normal partner. Instead I just consoled her with a sincere "That looks like it hurts."

After the exam I explained that the x-rays were negative, but that I was prescribing the use of an ankle support for several days. And yes, I would be giving her something strong for the pain. I left the room to finish the chart and write the script.

"Did you see her yet?" the charge nurse asked excitedly as I passed by her.

"See who?" I said.

"The lady I told you about. The medics said they just saw her over at St. Francis. She's working you for drugs."

"What? That lady?" I said incredulously. I remembered that the nurse had warned me that we had a "user" in the To-See rack. But not that lady. Surely.

"Yeah, I called over there. One of their nurses said she was just there and discharged with a script for Vicodin," she said, somewhat excited to catch someone red-handed.

"I think you've got it wrong on this one," I said. "She's just a nice little old lady. Besides she really has an injury." Now I was having conflicted feelings. I wanted to believe in the goodness of this person, but I didn't want to look like a fool to the staff. "I'll go straighten this out."

I went back into the room. Nobody else in the ER mattered at that moment. "I think there has been a misunderstanding," I started. "Have you been seen at another ER tonight?" I asked somewhat apologetically.

"No," she said defensively. Was this all a mistaken identity? I felt like I was accusing this fine lady because of somebody's jaded view of all mankind. But I was starting to get a knot in my stomach.

"Someone just told me they saw you in an ER across town," I confessed.

"Oh, yes," she explained, as a mother to a child. "I went over to St. Francis, but the wait was too long. I just left without being seen."

I was relieved. Now this was starting to make sense. *But what about the claim that she got Vicodin?* I really wanted to believe in her, even protect her. But my pride couldn't take having the nurses snickering about "Dr. Candy Man" all night.

"I'm going to get to the bottom of this," I said almost over my shoulder, as I ran to the nurses' station. "I'm sorry for any inconvenience but I'm going to call the other ER myself."

It's good no one was dying at the moment because when I returned to the nurses' station they were all gathered around like it was the OJ trial again. "Did you confront her? What did she say?" They were almost giddy with excitement.

"Call St. Francis ER. I want to talk to the doc that saw her. I think you have this all wrong," I repeated. I stood there as the nurse dialed the number.

"You actually handed her the script for twenty Vicodin?" I heard our charge nurse say to the St. Francis nurse before the doctor even came to the phone. I wheeled around and headed back to the room before the nurse could say any more. But I caught John the medic making the fishhook in the mouth sign.

When I got back to the room, she was gone. Someone in the hall said that her daughter had just wheeled her out. Without thinking, I raced to the waiting room and found her being wheeled through the revolving doors. *Take me for a sucker will you?* I jammed my foot in the door trapping them inside. "Ma'am you are not leaving until we get this straightened out," I shouted through the glass. I was glaring at them and she could see that I was angry.

"What were you thinking? What were you trying to do?" I demanded as soon as she got back to the room. I was the prosecutor and I was going to take nothing but the whole truth! Suddenly I saw all the things I had missed on the earlier examination—the trembling hands, the evasive eyes, the questionable injury. The staff was right about her and my fury mounted.

"I just didn't think that twenty pills were enough to get me through the holidays," she explained, attempting to retain her composure. "We just moved to town and I don't have a family doctor." That kind of statement would only make sense to an addict. Looking in her eyes, I still had compassion for her.

"Have you been taking narcotics for a long time and just didn't think twenty would last very long?" I was trying to give her an out.

"Oh, no. I've never taken any narcotic pain pills before," she lied. My heart sank. I wanted to believe her, but I finally had to face the fact that this sweet little lady was a narcotic addict or was supplying one. And what's more, she was a liar. It filled me with anger, embarrassment, and pity.

"Do you understand that obtaining narcotics through fraudulent means is a felony? That you can go to jail for this kind of thing?" I hoped she might come clean with me. Maybe I could at least help her with her addiction.

"Oh no," she insisted. "I would never try to do that." We were at an impasse. She couldn't or wouldn't see her problem. Her daughter was either complicit, enabling, or being duped like the rest of us. I just sat silently shaking my head as I tore up her prescription.

"Don't come back here," I finally mumbled as I slowly shuffled out of the room. There was a subdued silence as the lady was wheeled past the nurses' station. I couldn't look at her.

"You better call the other ERs in the area," I said, finally admitting defeat. "She's probably going to try somewhere else."

19

Nuts

THERE WERE NO PATIENTS TO BE SEEN when I walked down the hallway to get a cup of coffee. But when I returned to the nurses' station, Heather, one of the regular night nurses, was holding a chart and looking at me quizzically. "You have to see this guy," she said. "I don't have a clue what's going on."

That may sound funny. Of course, I have to see *all* the patients. But the nurses pride themselves on their patient assessments and they want to be able to tell me the diagnosis. As much as I try to get them to stop doing it, they attempt to give the answer instead of just giving me the facts. It's not that I don't want to know their opinion. I just don't want to be biased by their opinion before I see the patient. You can really put on the blinders and miss something if you go in expecting only to confirm the nurse's impression. So I found it rather refreshing for her to admit that she didn't know what was going on. *Now*, I thought, *let's see if I can figure out what really is going on.*

As I entered the room, I was surprised to find a skinny, middle-aged man contorted in such as way as to appear that he was almost tied in a knot. He was flexed at the waist with his chin down on his chest, even though his eyes were locked in an upward gaze. Remarkably, his left leg was almost over his head and neck. And both arms were stiffly extended into his groin with left hand actually shoved inside his pants.

My first impression was that the man was having a dystonic reaction. He had the unusual blank face of someone who had been on chronic antipsychotic medication. Sometimes patients with dreams of grandiosity or paranoia forget to take their meds for a while. Then they try to make it up by taking extra pills. The excess meds gives them the typical muscle contractions that make them appear to be tied in knots. Dystonia, locked up muscles, though serious, is easily treated. *I can heal this with a simple shot of Benadryl*, I thought. *I'll order the medication, cure the problem and be out of the room in less than two minutes. Then just sit back with a cup of coffee. The nurses will think I'm a genius.*

No, I thought further. *You can't be smug. You do that and they will be looking to take you down a notch. No, you have to be more subtle than that. You have to just reappear, put the chart in the orders rack, and appear busy. If they're talking, they will stop and say something like, "Boy, that didn't take long." But don't take the bait and start bragging about how easy the diagnosis was. You have to just let it sink in.*

Unfortunately, however, that wasn't it. As soon as I spoke to the patient my own visions of grandiosity quickly melted as he relaxed his upward stare and looked down as he easily raised his balding head.

"Hello, I'm Dr. Plaster. What can I help you with?" I started, somewhat disappointedly.

"You?...help me?" he said, reversing the question. Then he made a face at me like a little old man without teeth. He puckered his lips so much that it looked like they were out past his nose. I hadn't seen that expression since I was a little boy. Dickey, my friend, could do that. When we went to the swimming pool he could push his lips out so far that he could shut off the openings to his nostrils. It was cool, just like a porpoise. I was jealous because I had to hold my nose to go under water. It wasn't until I saw this man that I realized just how stupid he looked.

"It was an Act-o'God," the patient said, rousing me from my memories. "I've been prayin' about it. And nuthin's happnin.'" Then he made the Dickey face again.

I consider myself religious. So, unlike some of my colleagues, I don't always think that religious references are a sign of mental instability. But, I had to admit, this guy was starting to look like he had a few screws loose.

"What was an act of God?" I probed.

"My vast friends," he said, squinting his eyes and looking off into space while making his Dickey face. "I went to Harvard," he said somewhat triumphantly.

I wasn't sure whether he was a street guy and just delusional, or maybe he was one of those *Beautiful Mind* types who actually went to Harvard and just snapped. Regardless, time was starting to drag and I needed to cut to the chase.

"Have you been having feelings of depression lately?" I asked. "Have you had any thoughts of hurting yourself?" At least I would know if he was a potential admission.

"No!" he almost shouted. "Do you think I'm crazy?" We obviously had a difference of opinion on that matter.

He went on to try and explain but it wasn't making sense to me. I wasn't sure if I was just tired and not understanding him. But the more he explained the situation the more confused I felt. I could feel the conversation starting to wander. Finally, in desperation, I went back to my starting point.

"So...what *can* I do for you?" I said slowly.

"My vast friends, my vast friends!" he shouted now. He was starting to get frustrated with me. "I thought you said you're a doctor!"

Now I was getting frustrated, too.

"What's wrong with your friends?" I shouted back. "Are they chasing you?" *Maybe he's paranoid,* I thought. "Are you seeing people? Are you hearing the voices of your friends? Are you receiving messages from the dead?" I shouted the questions in rapid succession. I felt like I was on a game show and the clock was running out.

"Are you nuts, doctor? What are you talking about? I want you to look at my vast friends."

And at that he resumed the position he was in when I entered the room with his arms between his legs. But this time he reached into his under shorts and pulled out his scrotal sac. He took hold of his testicles with such a grip and pulled the sac so far away from his body that I reflexively winced.

"Whoa, there!! You are going to pull them off." Recoiling from the sight, it finally dawned on me what he was talking about. "Oh, you mean your *vas deferens,* part of the spermatic cord to your testicles."

"Yeah, that's what I said," he shouted, obviously relieved that he was finally being understood. Then he made that face again. "I thought you guys knew about this stuff."

Now he was making me feel dumb. I put on an exam glove and examined his scrotal sac. And to my chagrin, there was a swelling of his vas deferens. It could have been due to a resolving epididymitis, or just from chronic squeezing. Or it could have been a rare tumor. In any event, it was not an emergency. I was relieved to finally communicate, but frustrated that I couldn't fix the guys problem and look like a hero to the nurses. However, one thing was for sure; I wasn't going to get to the bottom of the problem tonight. I would just have to arrange a follow up with a urologist.

I began explaining what I knew of the problem, trying to reassure him as much as possible. But the more we talked the more disjointed his speech became. He was not just hard to follow. He had flight of ideas. I was not misunderstanding him. He was descending into a word salad. I was not the one in the room that was crazy. There was a larger problem here than his "vast friends."

"Sir," I began. "I think that you are having a little trouble organizing your thoughts. We have some special doctors here who…"

Before I could say anything further he stuffed his testicles back in his pants and jumped off the bed.

"You don't know what you're talking about, doc," he said with complete clarity as he started for the door.

I contemplated my options. He wasn't suicidal or homicidal. He wasn't even homeless. He needed help but he didn't want it. At least not from me. He was out of the room and headed for the door before I could get out the AMA form. It was useless to stop him.

"You were sure in there a long time," said Heather when I got back to the nurses' station. "What was wrong with him?"

"His nuts," I mumbled.

"He's nuts?" she fired back. "Is that all? I could have told you he was crazy before you went in there."

20

Exit Strategy

I FELT A LITTLE AWKWARD as the gray-haired man, every bit as big as me, draped his arms around my neck, laid his head on my shoulder, and wept loudly outside the trauma room. I stood stiffly. I had no words of comfort for him. His only son, a strong, handsome boy of eighteen, had just been declared dead by me. He was the victim of youth, speed, alcohol, and his own sense of invulnerability. The father's pain pierced through my shield of professionalism only briefly to wet my eyes, but I quickly put it aside, dealt with the issues at hand, and moved on to the next patient. I handled the reality of his loss the same as I always did. Don't get me wrong. I felt compassion for his pain. But death in the ED is a commonplace event. So death competes with distraction, fatigue, hunger, and intellectual curiosity. Sometimes it is simply one powerful experience among many.

When I was a kid one of my favorite games was playing war with my brother. And the best part was when one of us died. My brother was the best. He used to climb up on the dresser and let me 'shoot' him. He would then have a spectacular dive onto the bed, bouncing to the floor, followed by a long period of thrashing about as he died. He would always freeze in some funny position of "rigor mobus" as we called it. Like most kids, I had seen thousands of people shot, stabbed, and strangled on TV. And it looked like great fun. I suppose it could have turned me into some sort of sociopath. Instead it just made death feel very unreal.

Med school just reinforced this feeling. After my initial discomfort with dissection of a cadaver, I became very familiar with it. Like most med students, we gave a funny name to our specimen, ignoring the fact that the body we were cutting and probing had previously been a living person. And as the dissection proceeded, the body, and the person it represented, faded into its separate parts. The ugliness of death became completely lost on us.

We became much like the young marines that I encountered later in life. More than just watching violence on TV, they had grown up with high definition video games that tried to approximate the feeling of real warfare. Many desperately wanted to get into combat to see how it felt in reality. If they survived unhurt from a firefight they would be pumped up like a winning football team at halftime. But it all changed when one of their buddies was cut in half by an RPG. There was no chest bumping as they stood by watching a friend bleed to death from a gunshot to the neck.

Teenagers in general are like that. They are notorious for thinking that they will live forever. They consume poisonous amounts of alcohol and shoot things into their veins that were cooked in filthy spoons. I've grown accustomed to their blank looks when I've explained to teenage girls that their promiscuity is exposing them to unwanted pregnancy, disease, chronic pain, or sterility. Middle-agers are no wiser. Tell them that an airliner has a one in five chance of crashing and they would never think of getting on the flight. But tell them that their smoking has increased their chances of dying fivefold and they just ignore it saying, "Maybe it's just my time."

I once saw this sense of fatalism played out in all its grimness. After calling an end to a cardiac resuscitation effort on a man the same age as myself, I went to the grief room to tell his wife. Feeling a little closer to the situation, I braced myself for the wife's emotion and its impact on me personally. Entering the room, I found a middle-aged woman, plainly dressed, sitting all alone with a blank expression. I knew that she suspected the worst, but her reaction still took me by surprise. I informed her that we were unable to resuscitate her husband, saving the more stark statement for last: "I'm sorry to say that your husband has passed away."

I expected the dam of emotion to break. I reached out to comfort her. But there was no reaction. None. She sat quietly for a brief moment and then abruptly stood up saying, "I'll call the funeral home to come pick him up." The experience left me dull and lifeless.

It reminded me of an episode I had seen on Animal Planet. The narrator whispered to the viewers and the tension built as we watched a lion creep ever so slowly up on a herd of grazing zebras. Then, with an adrenaline explosion of violence, the lion made his move. The herd ran for their lives desperately as the lion singled out the weakest one for the kill. The viewers recoiled at the dying thrashing of the young zebra locked in the jaws of the lion. But when the young animal finally died, everything returned to a peaceful setting. The remaining zebras went back to grazing, virtually within sight of the lion devouring the kill.

I feel like I've done that sometimes. In the rush of a code blue there are shouts of orders. The orderly sweats as he pounds on the chest. Blood gushes from central lines and chest tubes. But then, it all seems to come to a dull end. The person that existed before just becomes a thing—the body—to be viewed, prepped, and disposed of. People resume their conversations, jokes, and stories. Life goes on. We immediately switch gears to other issues. I found myself even hurrying to get to lunch one day, before the cafeteria closed, almost forgetting to go to the grief room to tell the family of the death of their loved one. Another day. Another death. If it didn't involve any care I had rendered, the death of a person was of only a passing interest to me.

Is this how I'll die? I stopped to ponder one day. *Will some doctor who has a million other things to do pound on my chest for what seems an appropriate amount of time and then go back to doing what he was doing before. Will it just be another day, another procedure?*

Then I met Albert. That wasn't his real name, of course. It could have been Ralph or Ed. But he was anything but nameless to me.

When I picked up his chart I noticed that the chief complaint was "severe respiratory distress." But I noticed that he wasn't brought in by ambulance. Something didn't compute on this one. My first impression of Albert was that he was thin to the point of emaciation; his hands looked like skin stretched over a bony frame. With each breath, his thin shoulder muscles lifted his rib cage as if it weighed hundreds of pounds. His mouth gaped open to draw in the tiniest breath. His sunken eyes seemed to beam, though, like headlights shining from a cave.

"Call respiratory therapy and get a vent," I called out to a passing nurse. "We need to get ready for rapid sequence intubation."

"He doesn't want it," the young man standing at his side said with a grimace. "He's been expecting this for quite some time. And he has been clear that he doesn't want to be on a ventilator."

"I don't think you understand," I said impatiently. "He's going to die, right here, right now, or within minutes, if I don't intubate him."

"He knows that," said the young man whom I was beginning to realize was his son.

"I don't want to seem uncaring," I said, perplexed. "But why is he here then? Who brought him here?" I was anticipating a typical conflict. The dying patient doesn't want resuscitation, but the family loses their nerve to carry out the patient's wishes when the moment of truth arrives.

"He knows he's dying. But he asked me to bring him here. He said he didn't want to make my mom see him suffer like this. He said you guys are experienced at seeing someone die." Albert shook his head in agreement between gasps.

"I want to help you live, not help you die," I said to Albert with a tone of frustration. He simply reached out his boney hand and patted my hand paternally. I took a deep breath and sighed, almost as if my breathing was giving him air.

"He has end stage lung disease, as you can see," said his son. "He worked for years in the mines. His doctor sent him to a variety of specialists. But they all say that they have nothing further to offer him."

"Can I at least give you a little oxygen? It might help a little." I wanted to do something, anything. He only responded by continuing to pat my hand as if to console me. Then he gave a very slight smile. I tried to return it, but the sight was truly ghastly.

My mind raced to find something else to do, inside or outside the room. I asked a whole list of irrelevant questions, which the son answered calmly without taking his eyes off his father. I performed a cursory physical exam confirming what was already obvious, he was dying. With nothing further to do, I wanted to leave the room and resume some busywork at the nurses' station. But something held me at his side. I held his hand, or rather, he held mine as I stood on the other side of the bed.

"Are you sure you don't want me to do anything more?" I almost pleaded with him. Then he looked at me, gave that twinkle of a smile, and winked at me. He took one more gasp like a diver about to make a deep plunge... and died.

I didn't look to the clock to note the time of death, as I normally do to end a code. I didn't break for the door to write my note or resume seeing patients. I just stood there holding his lifeless hand, contemplating the moment. Something had just happened that I didn't understand. A man had stared death in the face and winked. But more than that, the life that he had exuded, even in the moment of dying, seemed to still be present. His son was different. I was different. More alive. More human.

I finally left the room to find any other family members to inform them of his death. But the grief room was empty.

"Oh, there's way too many people to fit in there," the charge nurse had informed me. Opening the door to the waiting room I was confronted by a huge number of people, some pacing, some sitting quietly. The crowd silently parted to make a path to a little old woman seated in the corner. She had the same twinkle in her eye that I had seen just moments before. Having nowhere to sit beside her, I simply took one knee to be at her level. I took her hand and introduced myself. But when I started into my standard spiel of "We did all we could do, but..." my throat tightened and a tear leaped from my eye. She took my hand, patting it gently as her husband had done. I couldn't say he had died. I just shook my head as if to say No. She smiled patiently and nodded her head yes.

After a long moment I rose to answer questions from the family. But instead of the usual "Did he suffer?" questions, they each in turn told their story of this great man's love, kindness, hard work, humor, gentleness, and on and on. One told of him taking his Saturdays to help them rebuild their worn-out kitchen. One teen told of being saved from an unjust punishment by his understanding intervention. After a long period that left me feeling refreshed, the charge nurse finally appeared at the door, signaling that I needed to get back to work. I knelt one more time to console Albert's wife. But this time she pulled me to her face and kissed my cheek. "Thank you for helping him," she said.

I returned to the rush of the ED, but never really left the spirit that was in that waiting room. When it was time to go home, I cleaned up the last charts and headed for the car. *Is that what it's supposed to be like?* I asked myself.

My drive home led me through long quiet stretches of highway with the Delaware wetlands stretching for miles on either side. As the fog rose to filter the morning sunlight I came to my answer. As gruesome as it might have seemed on the surface, I wanted to die like that man. I wanted to be able to look honestly at all the ugliness of death and still wink in sly defiance. Now I just needed to figure out how to live like him.

SECTION II
In the Desert

21

I Want YOU

LIKE SO MANY LONG AND FRUSTRATING nights, I found myself watching the clock as 0700 approached. The last few patients really tested my patience. One guy had his girlfriend on the gurney with him when I entered the room. They were laughing softly. He was obviously in no distress. His emergency was that he had missed work last night because of "back pain." And even though he had no pain now, he wanted me to give him a work excuse. Nothing more. *Heck,* I thought, *my back aches worse than yours. But, of course, that's because I WORKED ALL NIGHT! Is this what I trained for?*

After the shift was over, something caught my eye as I passed through the call room: a recruiting poster for Navy Reserve Medicine. The young officers looked sharp in their crisp white uniforms. My mind went back twenty years to when, after medical school, I had gone through the military match for residency training. My father and uncles had all served in the Navy, so it had seemed like the right thing to do. To my excitement, I had been matched to Tripler Hospital in Honolulu, Hawaii. But at the last minute, I backed out and took the safer route in a civilian hospital. As my mind drifted off into all the what-if's, I noticed that someone had revised the recruiting poster: "Qualifications, physicians up to age 35," had been inked through and now read, "Up to age 45." I was forty-nine. Practicality and Adventure waged a war in my weary brain.

"Don't even go there. You're too old," said Practicality.

"Somebody needs to do it," shrugged Adventure.

Like a kid stealing candy, I looked around the empty call room and ripped the poster down, hiding it in my lab coat pocket. When I got home my mind was racing. I sneaked into my office and started typing a letter. To my chagrin, the address on the poster indicated that the recruiting officer was a young woman. I could just envision her reading my letter. "Please don't laugh when you see my birth date," I wrote. I didn't tell my wife when I sealed, stamped, and dropped the letter in the mailbox. As I drifted off to sleep that morning, I dreamt alternately of winning the Congressional Medal of Honor and the horselaughs my letter was receiving in the Navy Reserve recruiting office.

Days later, when I had returned to my old self, I got the call. Her soft voice was businesslike and she addressed me as "sir," which accentuated the chasm between our ages. I was stunned when she said: "Yes, the navy will consider you if you are in good health." She would send me the paperwork and set up the physical exam. Assuming I passed, I would be commissioned within ninety days. I was high on Adventure.

"What are you doing?" screamed Practicality. "Have you thought about mentioning this to your wife? You don't need to worry about getting killed by some enemy—your wife will do it for them when she finds out."

Convincing the navy to consider me had been the easy part. I even passed the physical with flying colors. "You are disgustingly healthy," the examiner said, emphasizing the adjective as he finished the evaluation with a rectal. Driving home I realized I was finally going to have to face my family and friends. *Why was I really doing this?* I knew my wife would accuse me of having a midlife crisis. I was afraid my son, who was finishing four long years of training at the Naval Academy, would think I was a poseur, wearing the uniform without making the sacrifices it symbolized. But the biggest accuser was me: *You're old enough to be the father of most of these guys. Some guys are retiring before you ever enter.* I thought about it and prayed long and hard.

What came out of it surprised me. Citizenship. This is a great land we live in. Though not perfect by any stretch, it's a good land and I love it. And we all do our part to make it what it is. Some people make cars while others teach school. But we are all able to do what we want because someone stands between us and those who would do us harm. And the people standing in the gap are our sons, daughters, husbands, and wives; and they deserve the best we can give them.

"But why me? Why now?" asked Practicality.

Then I remembered my son's words the night before he left to report to the navy.

"You do know," my wife had asked him as a final gut check, "that this means you could be called to war sometime?"

"That's true," he said soberly. "But whose son would you rather send?"

Actually, in the end Practicality made the best argument for joining. After having been in the urban wars for years, I had more experience with 'combat' wounds than one would think. But now I would have a chance to help the people that have been laying their lives down to protect us. Surprisingly, all my family and friends seemed to understand. The old—and I mean old—guys at the coffee shop were openly envious that I was able to get into the military. Sixty years earlier, they had been in the position of the young men that I would now have the chance to serve. I told them I was honored.

My wife eventually let me sign all the paperwork, and there was a ton of it. I was shocked to find out how little is paid to those who risk their lives for us. Despite its informality, taking the oath and receiving the commission were both sobering and inspiring. The first time I went to put on my uniform was a little embarrassing. I felt like I was back in the Boy Scouts. The pants were too tight. I didn't know whether this was one of those instances of government vendors cutting corners or just me getting fat. I wasn't even sure whether I had the right insignia. Finally, when I thought the coast was clear, I stepped in front of the mirror to face the brutal truth.

"Hey, you look pretty hot," I heard my wife say softly as she passed.

"Really?" I replied, sucking in my gut. Maybe this was the right decision after all.

22

Nothing to Fear, But...

I DON'T KNOW IF IT WAS THE FATIGUE of the night shift or just the early morning Delaware fog, but I seemed to be in a dream as I made the long drive home. "Don't forget what today is," the medic at the ambulance doors had said. "It's 911 day."

"Oh, yeah," I had responded dumbly. *Was it some sort of EMS Appreciation Day or something? Maybe I'll do something special for the guys tonight. I have to be back in twelve hours anyway.*

I was almost asleep in the shower when my wife burst into the bathroom with a look of terror on her face. "Terrorists have crashed 747's into the World Trade Center towers!" I raced from the shower wearing only a towel. For the next several hours we sat with the rest of the nation watching in real time as the towers fell, the Pentagon burned, and our sense of national security vanished. With each new revelation of potential terrorist threats my sense of dread deepened. *How many more would die in senseless suicide bomb-*

ings? Were weapons of mass destruction in the hands of madmen? Was the clock of apocalypse ticking? I wanted to cover myself with the white coat of the ER doc who can face anything. But I felt naked, cold, and vulnerable.

I so wanted to have the faith of the little girl that I had seen recently. Having collided with the coffee table (a perennial culprit behind ER visits), she had sustained a wicked laceration to her eyelid. I was confident I could do an excellent repair with just a topical anesthetic if only she would hold perfectly still. But the thought of working close to the eye of a thrashing three-year-old gave me pause. I explained the situation to her father and began the discussion of using conscious sedation. But he interrupted.

"You will not need to strap her down or sedate her. She will hold still," he explained. I didn't believe him. I had sewn up my own kids at this age and it had always been a wrestling match.

As I prepared the suture tray, the nurse stood by with the papoose board for restraint in case things went south. But when the time came for me to begin sewing the child's laceration, the father gently took her from his lap and laid her on the gurney. She seemed so tiny in comparison to the bed. Her father simply looked in her eyes and said softly, "Hold still. The doctor will not hurt you. I will be here." She reached out and held his hand as he bowed his head to avoid seeing what I was about to do.

In stunned silence I worked on her eyelid, placing suture after tiny suture, without so much as a twitch from her. No, that's not true; twice she opened her eyes and carefully looked to see if her father was still there. It was as if the touch of his hand had grown numb and she wanted other confirmation of his presence.

When I finished the procedure the father thanked me profusely as he drew his baby back into his arms. But she acted as if nothing had happened. And soon she was running through the department, peering under curtains and making a cute nuisance of herself.

After the events of September 11th, I wished I could be like that child—reaching for and receiving assurance that everything would be OK. But what I got was the dissonance of commercials telling me to go on with my life as usual while news stories warned of being prepared for the "mother of all wars."

Then I met Joshua. He seemed more like me.

At ten years old he was stranded between feeling like a little boy and being expected to act like a young man. He had been pitched over the front of his bike, sustaining a jagged laceration to his lip and face. He was too big for a papoose and sedation was out of the question. He would simply have to hold still. I could tell that he wanted to be brave, but the increasing tremor in his hand and the terror in his eyes let me know that he could break at any moment. I could see that the protective instinct of his mother was making things worse. So I demanded that both parents leave the room.

When I turned back to Joshua he had his eyes clenched tightly and was about to erupt in a convulsion of tears. As I towered over him I took his face in my hand and commanded him sternly to open his eyes and look into mine.

"You do not need to be afraid of me," I said slowly and firmly. "Look at me. I will help you get through this. I won't tell you that there will be no pain. But it is not as much as you fear. Do exactly as I say. We will work together to get through this. OK?" After a long pause he took a deep breath and nodded silently.

The tremor remained, but the terror subsided. With each warning and needle prick his faith grew until he finally relaxed and allowed the repair to proceed without resistance. When all was finished he was making brave jokes to the nurse as I stepped out to speak to his parents. They had overheard my stern talk with their sweet boy. The mother was still hurting for him, but the father was pleased that their son had passed the testing of his fears. As Joshua came out of the room his bravado melted slightly as he approached his mother.

"How was it?" she asked, reaching out to him.

As he fought back tears of relief, I overheard him whisper, "I think I'm getting a little bit braver."

It would be a new world for us after September 11th. Our son was graduating from the Naval Academy into a mother's worst nightmare. And I had just signed up for the reserves. No one knew what to expect, but we assumed there'd be war. I trembled inwardly as I held my wife's hand. Finally I simply reminded her of what I'd said to Joshua. "We will work together to get through this. OK?"

23

Drill

AFTER REAMS OF PAPERWORK, I was officially in the United States Navy Reserve. I had the commission of my study on the wall to prove it. But this was going to be my first drill weekend. My orders were to report to the National Naval Medical Center in Bethesda, Maryland, at 0700. Walking out of the house in the predawn darkness, I was glad no neighbors could see me in my fresh-out-of-the-box uniform. I still felt that I didn't deserve the respect of the rank for which so many others had labored years to attain.

As I approached the hospital I couldn't help but be a little awed by its immensity. *It's just like all the other hospitals you've worked at over the years,* I reassured myself.

Well...not quite. As I drove along the driveway, I encountered a guardhouse from which emerged a marine with an M16 rifle. He was actually very polite. But I noticed my hand was shaking a bit as I showed him my orders and driver's license.

"I'm a newly commissioned officer," I murmured, fumbling with the paperwork.

"That will be fine, sir," he responded promptly, snapping to a sharp salute. I panicked. *What am I supposed to do? Salute him back? I'm sitting in a car for crying out loud...Nobody told me about this!* I caught a brief look of exasperation on his face as he held his salute. Finally I zipped up the window, scratched my eyebrow, and sped off, trying feebly to cover all the options in the same motion.

When I got to the ED I felt right at home again. I asked where the unit was gathering and was directed to a large waiting area by the unit clerk. Unaccustomed to military punctuality, I was about to learn my first lesson: 0705 is not the same as 0700. The unit was already lined up and the commanding officer was about to address them. I tried to slip in without anyone noticing. A man in enlisted uniform stepped forward and barked "Dress right!" Everyone seemed to look in my direction so I assumed he was shouting at me. I began anxiously examining my uniform. Then, just as he gave another bark (it sounded like someone had done the Heimlich maneuver on him), I felt the right elbow of the man next to me gouge my side. Everyone was taking tiny steps to the right. *Ohhhh, so that's what he means.* I was really beginning to feel out of place.

The CO's remarks were gracious in welcoming me to the unit, but I could tell that something wasn't quite right. I was informed that I would need to go to indoctrination. Another officer new to the detachment, a nurse, would be in the class with me. We were shown to an empty classroom by a courteous enlisted man. But as soon as the door closed, the nurse, apparently accustomed to orienting clueless doctors, said, "Sir, may I give you a little help with your uniform?" She quickly began removing and replacing all the insignia that I had only hoped to place in the right locations. Somehow I had succeeded in getting every part of my uniform wrong. It felt like I was in an episode of *Gomer Pyle*.

After several hours of indoctrination class (involving several more forms and a short test), we all gathered in a large auditorium to hear speeches by some high-ranking officials. With the mental stress of the morning and the warmth of the uniform, along with the droning speaker, I soon fell fast asleep. I don't think I snored, but every time a speaker finished everyone jumped to attention, leaving me slumped in my chair. If they were up I was still down; if they were sitting down, I was just standing up. I was hopeless. At lunch, I called my son, an ensign in the real Navy, and began relating the events of my morning. He was appalled that I hadn't been kicked out already.

Finally, the afternoon sessions were all medical lectures on topics related to what we could expect to see in the event of war. They talked about donning thick rubber chem/bio suits in one hundred–plus degree weather and caring for soldiers with burns, poisoning, and massive trauma. I began to wonder, *Why does anyone expose themselves to this kind of hardship? The pay is minimal and the risks are significant.* Then I felt a familiar swell of pride as they talked about emergency medicine being the first line of defense in the event of an attack. I remembered why I went into emergency medicine in the first place. It wasn't about money; it wasn't about the adrenaline rush (even though that was an attraction); it was all about being in a place where one could truly make a difference.

Driving home after the weekend I stopped at a freeway coffee shop for a dose of caffeine. I noticed the stare of a kid with green spiked hair and multiple piercings. I didn't know what he thought of this middle-aged guy in a military uniform. I just knew there was a good chance that someday he would need someone, somewhere, to step up and help protect him. And that person, whoever he or she was, would be a friend of mine.

24

In the Desert

WHEN I WALKED UP TO ALPHA Company's Shock Trauma Platoon (the marines' version of a mobile emergency department), I didn't even notice the commander who was sleeping on a litter under some camouflage netting that served as the triage area. The ambulances were lined up in front of the STP and the staff was sitting in the treatment tents. There were no patients. It was well over one hundred degrees and the netting provided the only semblance of relief from the heat. My friend, the other emergency physician from my unit, introduced us both to the corpsmen in the treatment tents as "the docs that would probably be relieving Alpha Company." We had arrived in the country soon after the cessation of hostilities and it looked like all the action was over. One young marine was assigned the task of giving us a tour of the facilities.

"What was it like?" I asked, sounding like a schoolboy on a field trip. Having been there for about a month, Alpha Company had handled the brunt of most of the battlefield injuries in this region.

"We saw about a thousand patients and did hundreds of emergency surgeries," he said over his shoulder as he proudly showed us the six-bed unit that was made up of two tents joined at the side by a walkthrough. It looked like your average ED, except that it had no monitors, pumps, pulse oximeters—virtually none of the electronics that we had come to rely on. Oh, and the dust. There was a thick layer of dust on everything. But that was understandable. After just a few days in this environment, I had sand and dust in every crevice of my life. It was inescapable. But as soon as I saw the patient board I felt at home—that well-worn, dry erase, patient-tracking board by which I had organized my life for the previous twenty years. Beyond the familiar tracking symbols this one featured the heart-breaking abbreviation, KIA.

"How does your system work?" I inquired after a moment's reflection on my own son returning safely from duty in the Gulf. *Let's get down to business,* I thought. *I'm a long way from home and I'm just getting started in this hellhole. I can't think too much about this.*

"The LZ for the choppers is over there, and they are loaded onto the ambulances and off-loaded here," our young guide continued. There was a tall berm of dirt and sand that separated the STP from the landing zone for the helos. It had only one entrance that was guarded by numerous guard posts with large caliber machine guns. Not only did this system provide security, it prevented even more of that nasty, tooth-coating dust from being blown into the treatment areas.

"How many patients can the helos bring at one time?" I asked, trying to get a feel for the pace of work.

"If they're serious, you might only get three or four at a time," he replied nonchalantly. "But if they can sit up, the helo holds sixteen. Then again, if they are EPWs they have to have marine security with them."

"We medevac enemy prisoners?" I was thinking of the cost of an aero-medical evacuation helicopter back home.

"Sure, we probably saw as many EPWs as we did marines. But they have to be under marine guard at all times. Most of them are happy to be out of the fighting. But a few, the fedayeen fighters, mostly jihadists from Syria, the ones with the scorpion tattoos, they'll try to kill you even while you are trying to save their lives. Be careful with them. In any event, it can get really crowded in the treatment areas."

"Did you treat them the same as our guys?" I asked somewhat incredulously.

"We treat our guys first, of course; but yeah, they get the same treatment as everybody else. Unfortunately though, many times we only got to them after their own guys had abandoned them. We had one guy who died from a single gunshot wound to the lower leg. He was discovered the day after a firefight. It looked like he'd been out in the field for over twenty-four hours, just bleeding to death..." The young marine shook his head. "If that had happened to one of our guys, a medic would have stopped the bleeding, shipped him out, and in a few days he would've been good to go."

We went on with our tour, peeking in the ORs—tents that were set up with operating tables and large green canisters with operating equipment. Despite being sealed tightly, the OR tents were just as dusty as anything else.

"We saw a lot of amputations from mines. They often came in twos. The enemy seemed to plan it that way. One marine would step on a mine and go down. When his buddy came to help, he would step on another mine placed near the first..." Our guide trailed off. It seemed like a particularly vicious tactic to take advantage of the marines' well-known practice of caring for one another.

"And that's the pharmacy, lab, and x-ray," he continued pointing to three other tents. The area between them was covered by cammie netting making for a sort of shaded hallway. The tents themselves were open in the front and gave the impression of a carnival sideshow. "The ICU's back there, but we didn't use it much. We recovered them as quickly as we could and sent them on to hospitals in the rear. The EPWs were mainly sent to the Comfort."

I was familiar with the navy hospital ship, USNS Comfort. It was a massive top-of-the-line hospital ship. It was fully air-conditioned with every treatment capability of a major teaching hospital in the States. "I can only imagine what some of those EPWs must have thought," I mused.

"Yeah, many of them were starving in the field. This was the first bath and hot meal they had gotten in months."

"Do you know what the plan is?" I hoped the young marine might have some inside information. "Are we supposed to take over here and let you go home?"

"I wish, sir, but I don't think so," he said dejectedly.

I had heard that our mission was to cover the exit of troops from the field. But nobody seemed to know for sure. "I guess all the fighting is over now," I said hopefully. It had been days since we had received any news. The only information we got was from the BBC on a short wave radio.

"We hope so," he said. "But don't count on it." The look in his eyes revealed fatigue and homesickness.

"Any suggestions for us?" I wanted any advantage I could get.

"Yeah," he said without hesitation. "Work the night shift. That's when all the best cases come in…and it's not so hot."

25

Hurry Up and Wait

GROWING UP, I HAD HEARD my father refer to his World War II experience with the timeworn adage of "Hurry up and wait." And one might expect that my experience in emergency medicine would have provided me with an appreciation for that concept. But it took me months in a barren wasteland to really understand.

When we arrived in the desert it was hot in the afternoon but pleasant at night. Located somewhere on the Iraq/Kuwait border, our camp was completely surrounded by sand. Or, more accurately, dirt—miles and miles of fine, powdery dirt. Each time the helicopters landed they kicked up huge clouds of dust. The marines had been nicknamed Devil Dogs since the First World War, but out here our unit became known as the Dust Devils. Dust got into everything: the tents, the supplies, our clothing, our eyes, and even our mouths. And then it got hotter. Daytime temperatures routinely topped 120 degrees. Everyone sat around like lizards in what little shade there was available. Common sense would suggest that people strip off some of the heavy clothing. But the minimum mandated uniform consisted of boots, long desert utility pants and green tee shirts. To go outside the protection of the guarded camp, to get to or to deliver a patient, it was necessary to don a long sleeve shirt, body armor weighing close to thirty pounds, a Kevlar helmet and, of course, the ever-present weapon. Within minutes all clothing was completely soaked through with rivulets of sweat running into our boots. Stay out very long and we had to start pumping even more fluids than our daily requirement of six liters of water.

Arriving after the cessation of most of the hostilities, we did a lot of waiting. We would sit quietly for hours each day attempting to lower our metabolic rates. Those that weren't busy writing letters home were deeply absorbed in thoughts of family and loved ones. For some unknown reason, we went almost a month without receiving any mail. Security concerns prohibited using cell phones with international chips. So there we sat, hour after hour, day after day, waiting in silence. Frustrations boiled over from time to time. Canteens of water became too hot to drink. And just when it seemed we couldn't take it anymore, the sun went down and the temperature lowered to a pleasant ninety degrees. And then, of course, the patients would start arriving.

There were always the heat illness patients. Then we had dysentery sweep through our camp and those around us. As marines came through from the northern swampy areas we saw a few cases of malaria, mostly from soldiers who had refused to take their prophylactic medication because it made them nauseous or sun sensitive. Broken bones and dislocated joints of marines fighting each other in jest or contest were frequent. One evening of karate training yielded a fractured rib, fractured elbow, fractured ankle, and a compression fracture of the spine. And then there were accidents, lots of accidents.

One night we received a frantic call reporting two gunshot wounds from within the camp. No one had any details. Did we have a sniper shooting over the protective outer berms? When the first ambulance arrived we received a young marine with a large portion of his lower leg blown off. He was in hypovolemic shock from blood loss, but was not bleeding on arrival. After a quick assessment of the ABCs he was off to the OR to have his wound cleaned and debrided. The next patient's face was covered in blood and dirt. But he was talking to us as if nothing had happened. He seemed a little confused, but we certainly considered that understandable.

After an ABC evaluation we began scrubbing his face and were surprised to find a single small entrance wound in his left temple. As his face started to swell and his level of consciousness dropped, it became clear that he had a penetrating brain injury. But a bullet seemed unlikely. A quick but crude X-ray revealed a metallic fragment in the left temple. Although we were a surgical hospital we had no neurosurgical capabilities. He had to be flown to a higher-level facility as quickly as possible. We had barely finished the rapid sequence intubation when we heard the rotors of the arriving Blackhawk helicopter. Running with him through the turbulence of the rotor wash, we lost the airway briefly. But once aboard the Blackhawk I was able to secure it again. I said a prayer of thanksgiving. Reintubation aboard the chopper would have been a challenge to say the least. Riding through the night sky I realized that the medic and the pilots were all around the age of my son. I had simultaneous feelings of protectiveness for them and honor to be among them.

We arrived at the tertiary care hospital, a huge complex of tents like our own, just as the patient's level of consciousness was starting to bottom out. A CT scan (yes, they actually had one) and a quick evaluation by a pleasant neurosurgeon (yes, they do exist), and we were off to the OR. I dropped my helmet, flak, gun, and ammo belt outside the room and watched as the craniotomy proceeded just in time. The brain was starting to bulge through the entrance wound, the bone was elevated and the dura entered. Slowly the destroyed tissue and the metal fragment were removed and the bleeding controlled. My patient would do well but his friend would end up losing most of his leg.

By the time I made it back to our unit, things had settled down for the night. The sick had been admitted to the wards and the corpsmen were lying about in the back of ambulances or on cots under the vast sky. In the stillness I walked through the group of sleeping strangers that I had come to call family. It felt like the times I walked through my children's rooms after a long night at the hospital. I said a prayer, thanking God for them and all they were doing. And then I, too, found a spot under the expanse of stars and settled down to wait for morning and the next day's burning sun. To wait for the next wave of patients. To wait for the time when we could finally all go home.

26

For Such a Time as This

THE CORPSMAN FROM THE BATTALION AID station was beyond duly respectful as he left. I had done nothing but reassure him that his care for the minor wound of his comrade had been appropriate. Perhaps a little education had taken place, but he had acted as though I had pulled his fat out of the fire. I should have been grateful to be so appreciated. But I was feeling sorry for myself. It had been a long, hot summer, and we had a long way to go before thinking about returning home. The idealism of the spring had burned off in the heat of the desert sun. *The truth of the matter,* I told myself, *is that I'm wasting my life in this God-forsaken place.* It seemed like I'd seen nothing but sunburn, lumps, and bumps. I had wanted to be a hero, but I was mired in the quicksand of a thousand meaningless tasks.

I was singing a familiar tune. For years I'd sung it any time I felt like I was trapped in the mundane events of life. Like most emergency physicians,

I tend to have a very low threshold for boredom. Give me an ED full of life-threatening trauma and I'd be in my element. But after a long night shift with nothing but sniffles and backaches, I'd feel depressed.

I was still wallowing when the petty officer handling the radio ran up and shouted, "We're getting a marine who fell off the palace, sir! He'll be here any second!" I began running to the triage area beneath the camouflage netting. Almost immediately I heard the ambulance drive up. The shouting outside told me this was going to be serious.

My 'emergency department' was in a CBPS, a chemical biological protective system, which was simply a special ambulance that had a large self-inflating tent attached. It was intended to treat chemical and biological warfare victims in a sealed environment. But my twelve-by-twelve space was the only really clean area for miles around, so it doubled as the ED. A patient would be passed through an airlock tube to where we could receive him. So when the trap door to the airlock was opened it was not unlike all the times I'd stood beside ambulance bay doors waiting for them to reveal the next challenge. *This is why I'm here!* I thought.

But not that night. It was not to be. As soon as I saw his face I could tell that the light of life was gone. What was the history? A watch post located high atop the palace. A simple misstep. Without a sound, in a heartbeat, he had fallen the lethal distance. We tried everything in the book to bring him back: intubation, IVs, chest tubes, CPR. But we all knew the result before we started. There would be no heroes that night.

After the pronouncement of death I sat staring at his young face. At nineteen-years-old, in top physical condition, he was the ideal marine. He'd had his whole life ahead of him, and then it was over before it had begun. I was ashamed of my self-pity. As I went outside into the darkness I wept for him and his family. I wept for myself. I wept for the utter wastage of life. *Why am I here?* I prayed as I lay down to sleep that night. I looked across the tent that I'd come to call home. I looked at my three colleagues, two trauma surgeons and an anesthesiologist; they had become like brothers to me and shared in my frustration. They were some of the best in the country at their trade. I saw the trauma surgeon pore over volumes of medical literature day after day, preparing for the cases that never seemed to come. It seemed the military was spending millions of dollars to have us just sit and wait...

I was deep in dreams of homecoming when the corpsman came running to our tent and shined a flashlight in my face. "Commander Plaster?" he sounded apologetic. "I need your help with a wounded marine. He's been hit by an RPG and is bleeding pretty bad."

I jumped off my cot, threw on my salt-stiffened utility pants, shoved bare feet into my boots and guided two marines carrying a third through the darkness to the CBPS. The wounded soldier was pale with blood soaking the battle dressing on his posterior knee. His leg, distal to the dressing, was pale, blue, cold, and tensely swollen. A quick assessment of his ABCs showed me that A and B were fine; but if we didn't quickly get control of his circulation, we were going to lose him. And if the bleeding didn't get him, he was going to lose his leg to a compartment syndrome. With multiple shrapnel wounds, it was clear that one of the fragments had gotten the major vessel of his leg. IV fluids, blood, pressure dressings, pain meds, and antibiotics—all came without much more than a word. My team was as experienced at this in war as I was in civilian life. In a matter of minutes we were ready to turn the case over to the surgeons.

My offer to scrub in and do whatever I could was gratefully accepted. The anesthesiologist did a rapid induction as the rest of us scrubbed and prepped the leg. Moments later the marine's leg was incised from mid-thigh to mid-calf relieving the compartment syndrome and revealing a large metallic fragment. In a matter of minutes the transected artery was exposed and shunted. The distal clot was removed. And the cold, pale foot started to pink up.

"We can do the vein harvest here," said one of the surgeons, "and fix this thing once and for all. Or we can quit while we're ahead, send him up the road, and let the army guys get the credit for saving his leg." Everybody knew that our surgeons were as capable as anyone in the country to do the arterial anastomosis. But we also knew that this was a field hospital. His best chance for a clean repair was at the army hospital.

"I say we ship him," said the lead surgeon humbly, knowing that he could be criticized for the decision. "We've done what we were put here for. Let's not go for the gold and screw this thing up."

I had become one of their greatest admirers and I wanted these two fine men to receive the credit for this save after all their waiting. But they only thought of the marine. We packed the wound and packaged the patient as the helicopters spun up on the LZ. He was starting to emerge from anesthesia as we lifted off. Flying in almost total darkness to prevent being spotted by surface-to-air missiles, I struggled to keep his airway secure, keep him sedated, and protect the tenuous shunt carrying blood to his wounded leg. I feared that if he awakened in the darkness with excruciating pain he might pull the ET tube or dislodge the shunt and die before we could get to the ground. At that point a wrestling match with an incoherent patient would have been catastrophic. But I eventually got control of the situation and settled down to a smooth flight. The cranial flight helmets, with their noise control headsets, and the complete darkness made for a surreal atmosphere. The gunners on either side of the helo had face helmets with night vision goggles that allowed them to look out the open windows of the aircraft and see the enemy on the dark desert below. Each was wearing a flight suit with a row of tiny green lights on the waist belt. The total effect was that they looked like space creatures with massive guns. Through the open tail of the CH-46 I could barely make out the dark silhouette of the helo flying cover for us. Alone in my thoughts I could only ask incredulously, *Is this why I'm here? Has God and the navy conspired to make us sit out here in the desert, wasting our time for months, spending millions of dollars, just to save this kid's leg? Was it all for this?*

A few days later I received another case that needed to go to the army hospital. It was a frivolous case, but I was so bored that I jumped at the chance to fly there, even if we would only be on the ground for a few minutes.

Upon returning I found that life was back to its previously boring state. The anesthesiologist had invented some carpentry project, making a desk from scrap pallets. One surgeon was writing home while the other had returned to reading his textbook. Passing by, I casually announced, "Oh, by the way, the guys at the army hospital said that our marine did very well and that we probably saved his leg."

Without looking up, my friend dropped his eyes from his textbook just long enough to give a soft pump of his fist and whisper the answer to my question from the previous night: "Yes."

27

Father's Day

BACK HOME IT WAS THE BEGINNING of Little League season. Dads everywhere were getting out the baseball gloves. A game of catch can be a good way to get to know what's on a child's mind. Plus the basic skills become second nature. But some dads want to take everything to the extreme. Just tossing the ball becomes a coaching session, a detailed critique of every flaw in the pitching motion. An easy conversation becomes a critical analysis. A time of strengthening the body and affirming the heart can instead become a test of ability and a blight on a young soul.

I know this because I had a father that couldn't just play. He had to constantly correct. As a result I came to fear playful competition and failure. Nevertheless, I played every sport I could, desperately seeking my father's approval and hating him for withholding it. Over the years I thought I had gotten over my angst; I thought all the coaches in my life had beaten it out of me. But no, I passed this unholy blessing on to my son. That is until I saw the same fear in his eyes that I had known as a child. I vowed to God that this curse would stop with my generation. "Just let him play!" my wife would say. Finally I learned to do so. And ever so slowly I became the very thing that I desperately wanted to be: his hero.

I was thinking of that little boy, who was now a man and a naval officer, as I walked back from Sunday chapel. The chaplain's sermon, on this special day, was on fatherhood. The relative cool of the night was gone. The sun was already blazing hot and the temperature was sailing past 115 degrees. I was deep in thought when I got back to the area where our unit was camped. When I looked up I saw an ambulance with its backdoors open and a lot of people stirring about. It was a scene I had witnessed numerous times over the years.

"What's going on?" I asked one of the corpsmen sitting on the hood of the ambulance outside the treatment tent.

"A grenade injury, sir," he said jumping to his feet.

"Why wasn't I notified?" I demanded. I was the Officer in Charge of the STP and the only emergency physician. Nothing was supposed to happen without me knowing about it.

"I think the chief sent someone for you, sir. But they must have gone a different way. The patient just got here," he stammered somewhat defensively.

I hadn't meant to sound like I was attacking him, but it must have come out that way. When I entered the tent the first thing I noticed was a mangled foot. Everyone was basically ignoring it and working to start IVs for the man attached to it. He looked to be in his late twenties, muscular, crew cut, and obviously in a great deal of pain. His fists and teeth were clenched and his body was shaking. But the worn ring on his hand and a gentleness in his face spoke of fatherhood.

"What have you done so far?" I asked the blond nurse affectionately nicknamed "Cheesecake."

"He's gotten a gram of Ancef and ten milligrams of morphine," she said without looking up from the IV she was holding. She was all business. Her husband was a Cobra pilot and she was an experienced navy nurse. Just the sight of her was a comfort to most of our injured guys, and she came across like a sister to everyone.

"Did he lose much blood?" I queried while looking at the monitor for his blood pressure. I had seen some injured marines with large volume losses drop their pressures rather dramatically when their pain was relieved, so I wanted to have some frame of reference. What was left of his foot was covered with a black clotting powder that made it look like it had been overcooked.

"There was supposedly a lot of blood at the scene, but the corpsman got control of it right away," she said with more of the morphine poised over the IV.

"Go ahead and give him all the MS he needs. We'll chase his pressure with fluids if we need to," I said. I gave him a quick physical exam to look for other injuries, but he was already too sedated to answer any questions about how the injury happened. The OR was soon ready and we took him right in. After a quick induction, our two trauma surgeons set about amputating most of his destroyed foot. They were amazed that somehow he had managed to save his great toe and the ball of his foot. With a shoe prosthesis, he would probably even be able to run almost normally.

I went outside to let the commanding officer know of his condition and that we would be airlifting to another facility for more surgery and rehab. Over the CO's shoulder I noticed another soldier, around the same age, dirty and grizzled, pacing about anxiously with tears streaming down his face. "How did this happen?" I asked the CO.

"The terrorists around here are using kids," he said disgustedly. "The gunner's vehicle," he pointed to the other soldier, "it broke down and he wasn't able to cover the sergeant's back. Apparently some friendly kids approached the sergeant's vehicle and one of them tossed in the ordnance. He sacrificed his foot by pushing it up under the dash, but he saved the other guys in the vehicle."

I thought about my recent trip on the convoy through Iraq and all the children that would run to the road to greet the vehicles. Big smiles and thumbs up, hoping to get a little candy tossed their way. *Who would endanger a child's life like that?* I thought. If someone gave a kid a grenade, it could easily kill the kid as well as the intended target. The chaplain's warning of the responsibility of fatherhood rang in my mind. "If anyone should cause one of these little ones to stumble, it would be better for him that a millstone be tied about his neck and cast into the sea." The frustration of this war was welling up inside of me as I walked away from the CO.

"Is he going to be OK?" the anxious soldier pleaded. The OR crew had just finished bandaging the stump and I could hear the medevac helicopter arriving in the background. It wouldn't be long until we carried the patient past his friend.

"He lost most of his foot, and there is a lot more surgery to go through before we can know anything for sure. But the good thing is that it looks like they were able to save his big toe." I went out on a bit of a limb with that last one, but I wanted to give his friend a little hope.

"That's good. That's real good. Thank God," he said with a sigh. Then after a pause, "Do you think he'll be able to run?" He asked like a man trying to negotiate for one last favor. He knew he was pushing his luck, but he had to ask. "It's just, he's got two little boys at home. He thought he was going to lose most of his foot. But he said he would be good to go if he could just run with his boys and play a little baseball."

28

The Economy of Gratitude

I WAS BACK TO WORK at a hospital in the States, and it almost felt like I hadn't been gone. Iraq seemed like a distant memory clouded by dust and distorted by the wavy lines of heat. Eight months of my life seemed unaccounted for. People asked what it was like. "It was hell," I'd say. But actually it was more like Purgatory; not really Hell, but you could see it from there. Riding on the back of a seven-ton troop truck in 135-degree heat was like standing in front of a blast furnace for several hours. We all dreamed of going home, and we knew our loved ones were praying for the same. But it seemed unreachable. The "latest possible date" for going home kept getting postponed by weeks and months.

Different sights and sounds still took me back there. I didn't know if I'd ever be able to enjoy a thunderstorm again. My mind always returned to a pleasant telephone conversation I was having with my wife that was interrupted by three loud crashes. *Thunder?* That's odd, I thought. *It hasn't rained the whole time we've been here.*

Suddenly one of my marines stuck his head in the door and said respectfully, "Sir, we have to go to the bunkers." Ignoring him, I continued listening to Rebecca chatter about home. "Sir," he became more insistent.

Finally, I saw the distress on his face. "Uh, sweetheart, I'll have to call you back."

"You've got to hear this," she continued.

"Sir!" the marine finally shouted. "Get off the fuckin' phone! They're firing rockets at us."

"Oh, uh, yes," I said feeling foolishly naive. "Honey," I interrupted again. "I really do have to go. I'll call back. Uh, why? Well...the enemy is shooting rockets at us."

Silence on the other end of the line.

"I'll call back in a few minutes," I said trying to be nonchalant. "I just have to run to the bunker right now. I'll be fine. Hold that thought and I'll call you right back."

We spent most of that night in the bunker. It was six hours before I was able to return the call. From the depths of our hearts my wife and I thanked God once I was finally home safe.

At other moments my mind would slip back to the time I was walking through the killing fields of southern Iraq. A huge field had been freshly dug and was littered with garbage bags. The locals told of seeing truckloads of people brought to the area and summarily executed. The bodies of the dying and dead were pushed into a pit by a backhoe and covered up. Only when the Americans arrived did the locals feel safe to return to the field and dig up their loved ones. The bodies had been recovered and reburied properly. The bags contained all that remained of clothing and personal effects that would allow for family members to identify the unclaimed dead. As I walked through the field I noticed a small pair of shoes. They were the size of a young child. What caught my eye was that they were tied with rags rather than shoelaces, and that the socks were still in the shoes. As I examined them I thought of a mother who was looking for her son or daughter. My thoughts turned ghastly when I discovered that the child's feet were still in the socks.

Later, seeing the look of horror on my face as I left the field, my commanding officer addressed me. "I know you're a reservist and didn't have to come here. And at times you may even question whether you did the right thing. But someone had to come and stop this, and you raised your hand. And I, for one, want to thank you."

That small comment meant more to me than any of the medals I received for my service.

Any time I'd treat a football injury my thoughts would drift back to a nineteen-year-old marine that I treated twice. The first time I saw him he and his buddies were shouting excitedly to each other as they lay on gurneys in the Shock Trauma Platoon. They had been tasked with driving up a road as fast as they could at night to draw fire from a known ambush. Then the light armored vehicles with their Bushmaster machine guns would come in behind and destroy the would-be ambushers. This marine's vehicle had been struck by an RPG shell that had skipped across the windshield before exploding. Miraculously, he and his two buddies had suffered only minor shrapnel wounds and were high-fiving like they had just won a tough football game. They all refused to let their families know that they had been injured and returned to duty almost immediately. But two weeks later the same crew was brought back to the STP. This time an RPG had blown off the entire front of the hummer. The nineteen-year-old's face and eyes were bandaged, and he had shrapnel wounds covering the rest of his chest, hands and arms. Nevertheless he kept up the friendly banter with his fellow marines until his commanding officer came to check on him.

"What happened out there?" asked the colonel, whom I had gotten to know from the previous experience.

"I don't know, sir. They were shooting at us from both sides. The RPG took off the front of the hummer and the tires were shot out. I thought we were going to die..." His voice started to falter. "But Martinez just kept driving, sir. He saved our lives," he said, finally cracking to the flashpoint of tears.

"We need to send him to the rear for some x-rays and a consult with an ophthalmologist," I reported. The colonel was a tough guy and he tolerated no slackers. But in his eyes I could also see the look of a father who was breathing a sigh of relief that one of his boys had cheated death yet again.

"Oh, that's fine," he said without hesitation. "This will make this man's second Purple Heart. And I'm not going to let him try for three."

"Thank you, sir," I said with relief. "Thank you."

Gratitude. Isn't that the real currency of our profession? Of course, we like to get paid. But what we really hope for is a little gratitude. And the funny thing is that we all carry a pocket full of it, to give away if we will.

Sometimes these gifts of gratitude seem to come from nowhere. Like one did on a blistering Iraqi afternoon in late August. We had broken camp in a rush because we had received assurances from our command that we were on our way home. Convoys were grueling because of the heat and latent danger. In recent days I had witnessed six deaths from these seven-ton behemoths driven in close intervals and low visibility. Add to that the danger of inching through the crowded streets of small towns that all potentially harbored enemy combatants with scores to settle. Only days before an officer had been shot at close range while passing through a nearby town.

We took no chances. All weapons were on "condition 1," pointed outboard. All eyes were scanning every car we passed. That day I trusted my life to a nineteen-year-old from Indiana who drove a seven-ton truck with one hand on the wheel and the other on a nine-millimeter pistol. We arrived at our destination exhausted, filthy, and on edge. At the worst possible moment we received the crushing news that we would not be going home for another month. We felt betrayed. It seemed like I was barely hanging on to the knot at the end of a rope.

Then I saw two letters on a pile of overlooked mail. The names on the return addresses were total strangers, but each envelope enclosed a note to some 'faceless soldier' just to say thanks for what we were doing and to encourage us to stay the course. Simple gestures, but at that moment they struck me with overwhelming force. As I read the letters, the rivulets of sweat on my dirty face were joined by streams of tears.

After returning home it was surprisingly easy to slip back into the old feelings of being used by thankless patients and staff. Of course, this is my job and I get paid to do it. But we all depend on receiving a currency that is worth so much more. And now it was my turn to rejoin the economy of gratitude.

As I was leaving the ED one morning, I noticed one of the young custodians mopping the floor in an isolated treatment room. I had never really noticed him before, let alone caught his name. But this morning I spotted the eagle, globe, and anchor tattoo on his forearm. *So this kid's been a marine,* I thought. He seemed too young to have seen so much of life.

"Hey, Devil Dog," I said sharply.

"Yes, sir?" he responded, standing erect.

"You're doing a great job," I said, softening the tone of my voice. "This is the cleanest ED I've ever seen. You make our job of caring for patients possible."

"I do the best I can, sir," he said. I thought of all the others who would have given a similar response.

"I know you do," I said. "And I just want you to know that I appreciate it." Our eyes met as I turned to leave.

"Thank you, sir," he said softly.

No, I thought. *Thank you.*

SECTION III
Answering the Call

29

The Colonel

IN THE WINTERTIME IT SEEMS that the night shift fills up with drunks and bums trying to get in out of the cold. The savvy patients have learned that if they have complaints that can't be easily ruled out they will not be back on the cold streets for many hours. If the nurses are in a benevolent mood they might even get a meal in addition to the warm bed for the night. For them, even the long hours in the waiting room are no problem. But for some of the staff these patients are a personal affront. Night after night they present with what appear to be bogus complaints. They reek of alcohol, body odor, vomit, and urine. Many know how to play the system and are very demanding. Some, we find out to our surprise, have serious hidden complaints. But others just want to be warm and left alone. And then there are those we fight with, night after night, going through needless workups for imaginary problems.

A friend of mine told me about one patient who could barely drawl through his drunken stupor that his jaw hurt when he bit on anything. Examining his mouth, it was easy to see that his grossly carious teeth could be painful. But a compulsive young physician took an x-ray of the mouth. To his surprise he discovered a full knife blade embedded in the patients face behind the zygomatic arch. The doctor could only hypothesize that during one of his patient's previous drunken episodes he had been stabbed in the head with the blade breaking off in the soft tissues. A second examination of the skin anterior to the patient's ear revealed a fine, well-healed stab wound.

I still carry the scar of one encounter with a drunk. The local volunteer unit brought him in under the custody of the county sheriff. We could hear the swearing and shouting as the ambulance bay doors opened. The only history provided by the ambulance squad was secondhand from bystanders at the bar from which the patient had been taken against his will. The story was that the patient had been drinking all night at a local watering hole. After finally verbally abusing the wrong person and taking a wild swing, the more sober customer had clocked him in the mouth knocking him off his stool. The sheriff had been called to break things up.

When I saw him he had a fat lip, an abrasion to his elbow, and a very nasty disposition. He was in four-point restraints and snarling like a wild animal at anyone who got near him. He was threatening that when he was released from restraints he was either going to perform a variety of sexual acts on the nurses who were attempting to assess him or he was going to kill us all. We couldn't see anything but superficial injuries. Any attempt to examine his face or head resulted in the patient attempting to bite or spit on the examiner. He moved everything with full strength and was seemingly in no distress. While evaluating my next step, the charge nurse announced that a helicopter was inbound bringing a level I trauma patient. So I elected to watch him, let some of his booze burn off, and reassess him when hopefully he was less combative. I couldn't spare all the staff to hold this guy down while we did a thorough exam.

By the time the trauma case was taken care of, his mental status had declined from a snarl to a moan. Yelling and spitting was replaced by slow, deep breathing. A quick exam revealed a tiny scalp wound hidden in his thick curly hair that he had prevented us from examining previously. By then we were behind the curve. A quick CT showed me what I suspected but didn't want to see: a temporal skull fracture and a growing subdural hematoma. Neurosurgery was called and he was taken to surgery for evacuation of the clot. But the patient did poorly post-op and eventually died later in the ICU. Since he carried no identification the hospital could not locate any family or friends for days after his death. But when they finally did, his family members sued everyone involved in his care.

The plaintiff's expert said that I should have paralyzed him, put him on a ventilator and gotten a CT immediately. Maybe he was right. But I would have had to shoot him with a sedative dart before approaching him. Moreover, if I followed that credo I would have a house full of drunks on vents every night. And I'm sure that one of them would crash on me some time and then I'd get sued for that too.

So I guess one could say that I'm a little gun shy of drunks. If they said they had some problem I'd give them the full workup. It seldom revealed anything, but it gave the nurses something to do. Unfortunately it could also release something very disturbing. Drunks who were only a little obnoxious on arrival could go into a full-blown rage after they had been stripped, restrained, IV'd, and catheterized. As the patient's rage heightened some staff members would take a perverse delight in inflicting pain on the hapless victim. I usually tried not to get involved in the interpersonal conflicts of nurses and patients. But one time I did.

We had this old guy that would show up on an almost weekly basis. The complaint was always the same, chest pain. The workup was always negative. Week after week it was the same routine. As soon as one of the nurses announced "Bill's back," they would all swing into action. They would try to disrobe him. He would swear at them. They would attempt to hold him down. He would take a swing at one of them. They would get out the leather restraints. He would demand to pee. They would get out the largest catheter they could find. On and on it went. I often thought that if this guy ever really had a heart condition the workout we gave him would either shape him up or cause his death.

Finally, one night after we had "worked him up" for the umpteenth time, one of the nurses commented, "Did you know he was a Vietnam veteran?"

"Yeah," the orderly chimed in. "I heard he was decorated for bravery or something. His unit saw a lot of action."

"I've heard his family refer to him as 'colonel,'" added the nurse.

I stared at the scrawny old man. He was my age but looked twenty years older. Suddenly my eyes were opened and "Bill the drunk" became a man with a history. Sadly I had seen other veterans who seemed intent on blotting out their memories with alcohol.

The next time Bill came staggering into the ED I was ready to receive him. "Just leave me alone," the old man shouted as I approached his bed.

"Colonel," I said. He stopped and attempted to focus on me through his haze. "Sir," I said. "This is Lieutenant Commander Plaster. Are you OK?"

He eyed me warily, then mumbled, "I'm OK. Just leave me alone."

"I can't leave you alone if you are sick or injured. So I have to ask you: Is there anything wrong tonight, or have you just been drinking too much?"

"Why do you care?" he replied suspiciously.

"Because, sir," I said, "if you have a problem or an injury of any type, I'm glad to take care of you. But if you don't really have a medical problem, I won't bother you with any tests. If it's just the booze I'll let you sleep it off. I'll just check on you once in a while to make sure you're OK." I knew the risk I was taking, but this didn't seem to be about me.

"Oh," he said shaking his head. "I'm just an old drunk. I'm sorry for taking up space and bothering you."

"It's no problem, sir," I said. "I'm sorry we've mistreated you in the past."

His angry face had relaxed and his demeanor completely changed. Several times throughout the night I checked to see if he had any complaints whatsoever, but he was fine. He got up and left the following morning, sneaking out while I was seeing another patient.

In the subsequent weeks and months I noticed that his visits were becoming less frequent. And he was always apologetic about his condition. Then we didn't see him any more. I didn't know what had happened to him. I was afraid he had died. Then one day after Christmas he walked into the ED. He was clean-shaven and wearing old but clean clothing. And he was stone sober. He came with a small gift for the staff.

"I'm so sorry for all the trouble I've caused you good folks over the years," he said humbly. The staff was slack jawed.

"It's been an honor to take care of you, sir," I said, breaking the silence. After a long pause he turned to leave.

"Sir," one of the nurses said, smiling warmly. "You can come back any time."

30

Survivor's Guilt

I POSITIONED MYSELF CAREFULLY IN FRONT of the three-year-old. "Open wide and say 'Ahhh,'" I said. Looking over my shoulder, I noticed that everyone in the room had their mouths wide open, including me. Everyone, that is, except for the three-year-old. Were we coaching or identifying? I think it is a lot of the latter. But it's funny how our identity with the patients we treat changes over the years. I recall how, as medical students, we seemed to experience the symptoms of whatever diseases our patients had at the time. Twentysomething interns serving on cardiology rotations worried that the twinges in their chests were really the beginnings of life threatening heart disease. It didn't occur to them that they were running triathlons on weekends. Often we found ourselves weeping with family members of a dead patient we had met only minutes before. Their bodies were our own and their losses ours to grieve as well.

We all went into medicine to help heal people. And it seems at times that we really could feel their pain. Too much sometimes. And for many, the burden became too much to bear. Thoughts of patients with diseases for which I could do nothing would often plague my mind for days. And it wasn't just the fact that I couldn't help; it was the reality of irrevocable suffering.

Then something happened. As the successes of a medical practice and a young family flooded my life with joy, I disassociated myself from the pain of those I encountered each day. I compartmentalized the pain. I said to myself, *That's the ER. My life is different.* Sometimes I rationalized that the patients had brought it upon themselves. *I can't help it that they have smoked until they can't breathe any more. And that diabetes; isn't that mainly the result of out-of-control obesity? And how many problems would disappear from the ED,* I would think, *if there wasn't alcohol abuse?* I became detached. Not cynical, just detached. I wasn't like them. Psychiatrists would probably recognize this as a self-protective mechanism. And it probably is. Maybe it's necessary to do what we do. But maybe it's not.

My perspective began to change one night when I became a patient. I had just finished a long string of night shifts, and I was tired but still anxious to get started on a long-awaited vacation camping trip. A momentary lapse in judgment as I was hooking up the travel trailer to our minivan and I amputated the tip of my long finger. I walked into the ED of the hospital closest to my home. The triage desk was stacked with charts and the waiting room was packed. I knew a two-hour wait to be seen was not unrealistic. But I needed immediate help and I was, I felt, the exception to the rule.

"Hi," I said to the triage nurse while waving my bloody hand. "I'm an emergency physician and I can see that you are jammed tonight. But if someone could just give me a digital block right away, I'd really appreciate it." Her harried look said, *If you're so smart, why did you do such a dumb thing?* But to my eternal gratitude, she took me back to get my block.

Not long after my hand had healed and I was back working in the ED, I walked into a room to see a patient who had his hand soaking in a basin of Betadyne. His face was pale and his hand was quivering. "What happened?" I asked blandly. He grimaced as he lifted his hand out of the basin to reveal a crushed amputation exactly like my own. I felt my stomach tighten and my face flush. "How long have you been waiting?"

"About two hours," he responded numbly. "An hour in the waiting room and a hour back here."

"I am so, so sorry for this," I said with painful embarrassment, as my mind flashed back to the excruciating minutes that I had waited for my own pain relief. Something was different now. My perspective was beginning to change back to one of identity with my patients. But my mind rebelled. *I can't do this,* I thought. *I can't carry with me all the pain that I encounter in my professional life. It will rob me of any of life's joy. I won't do it.*

Then my life encountered Eric. He was the long-awaited son of a dear family friend. More than that however, he was the exact age of my own granddaughter who lived far away from me. He was my surrogate grandson. Two weeks before Christmas I got a call late at night to meet his parents in the ED. His initial presentation was rather benign, cold symptoms maybe. But soon it became clear that something much worse, something inexplicable was happening. We clung to the hope that it was nothing. But the truth became clear that he was born with an extremely rare genetic defect that, in the final analysis, was inconsistent with life. One moment I was the reassuring family friend, while the next I was the dispassionate clinician explaining with objectivity the horrible reality that they were facing. It was a schizophrenic time of pain and denial. After an eternal two-week struggle, Eric succumbed to reality and died in his mother's arms. Though I raced to the hospital when I heard the news, I wasn't there when he died because I was home playing with my granddaughter who was on a brief holiday visit.

Leaving the hospital through the ED, I saw the scared faces of many more patients wondering what fate awaited them. I couldn't look anyone in the eye. *How can I do this?* I asked myself. *How can I embrace such sorrow and tragedy while still enjoying even the smallest of life's joys?*

Three days later I stood at the graveside watching a tiny coffin get lowered into the frozen ground. Snow was softly falling. Recalling Eric's wry little smile as he lay in the isolette taking some of his last labored breaths, I soaked the front of my overcoat with tears. In the distance church bells were ringing *Joy to the World*. Like the first one thousands of years before, this was going to be a beautiful and terrible Christmas.

I heard a voice say, *Through some miraculous and timeless providence we are able to simultaneously embrace all the joy and sorrow that life brings our way. Sorrow does not have to steal from joy; it gives it meaning. And joy does not diminish sorrow; it only provides perspective and hope.*

Joy and sorrow—it's not a zero-sum game.

31

In the Middle

AFTER A LONG NIGHT OF RACING from one room to the next, I finally got to the bottom of the pile of charts of patients to be seen. I was looking forward to relieving the strain on my bladder and drinking a cup of coffee, in that order. When I looked at the complaint on the chart, I was both annoyed and relieved. The complaint was, simply, "Thinks he has VD." It really irritated me when people used the emergency department as a three AM convenience care clinic. But then I thought, *Since this clearly isn't an emergency I'll make quick work of this and send him to the public health clinic in the morning.*

"HELL-O," I boomed impersonally as I entered the room. A healthy-appearing young man, well groomed, was sitting on my stool and chatting on his cell phone. Being already irritated, this made me more determined to punt this guy out the door any way I could.

"So you think you have VD, huh?" I glanced at him over my glasses before plowing into the paperwork. If there was one thing I hated more than taking care of a frivolous complaint at three in the morning, it was doing all the infernal paperwork that came with it.

Unlike the old kind of medical note that only required the doctor to write a brief description of the case, the new charts consisted of pages of questions with blocks that had to be filled-in with answers. Block 1: *What time did I see this patient?* Block 2: *Did I review the nurse's notes and vital signs?* Block 3: *How does the patient rate their pain on a scale of one to ten?* I looked at all the questions on the template and my heart sank. I looked up to the ceiling as if to ask forgiveness in advance for the fraud I was about to commit, and then began filling in the blocks as fast as I could.

"So you think you have VD," I said again with my eyes on the chart.

"Well, I really don't think..." he started.

"Do you have any kind of drip or discharge from your penis?" I interrupted with my pen poised over the next box.

"Well, actually I don't really..."

"I guess you know that I have to get a culture," I interrupted again, continuing to madly make check marks. "And to do that I have to shove a Q-tip all the way up your..." I paused and looked at him. I wanted to make sure he understood the torture that was about to be inflicted. His eyes were wide open and he was cowering in the corner.

"You're going to push something up my...you know," he said looking down at his crotch and screwing up his face as though he'd just tasted formaldehyde. "Is it going to hurt?"

"It's going...to hurt...like Hell." I responded slowly, twisting the knife.

"But I don't even have a drip or anything," he whimpered. He looked like a kid about to take a whipping for something he didn't do.

I stopped. "You don't have a drip?"

"No," he almost squeaked.

"Well then, what makes you think you have VD?"

"I don't think I have VD," he said, pleading his case.

"Well, OK then…" I shook my head in confusion. "Why are you here?"

"My wife…" he started.

"Ohhh," I interrupted. "I get it! She was told she has an infection and now she wants me to see if you have one?" I was back on track and more irritated than before. This was not just a frivolous complaint; it was a frivolous non-complaint.

"No," he said softly.

"No, what?" I asked, looking up from the chart.

"No, she doesn't have an infection either," he replied.

I stopped again. "She doesn't have an infection and you don't have any complaints. So, why are you here?" I was back to where I started and my bladder was giving me the two-minute warning.

"She thinks I've been playing around on her," he explained.

"Have you been?" I squinted.

"No, doc, I swear!" He was holding his loins as if to make an ancient Hebrew oath.

I continued the cross-examination. "And you don't have any discharge?"

"No, I'm clean! I swear it, doc." He jumped to his feet and started to drop his trousers.

"That's OK," I said quickly. It was way too early for an unnecessary crotch examination. I looked over all the needless check marks. "Well, if you haven't been exposed and you don't have symptoms, I guess we don't need to do the culture."

"Will you tell my wife that?" he almost begged.

"Yeah, I guess. Tell her to come in and I'll talk to her." I'd started to feel sorry for the guy. He whipped out his cell phone and began dialing furiously.

"Hey baby, this is Michael," he was talking rapidly in a high-pitched voice. "I'm with the doctor in the emergency room and he says that he has to shove this big thing up my thing. But baby, I swear to you, I haven't done anything. Will you talk to him?" He thrust the cell phone at me.

I had barely introduced myself when she cut me off. "What are you talking about shoving up my baby's thing?"

"A...a...swab," I stammered. "Well, actually I don't have to do a culture because he says he doesn't have any symptoms. That is, as long as you don't have any signs of a sexually transmitted disease. And you don't have any symptoms, do you?"

"WHAT!" she shouted in my ear. "Sexually transmitted disease? Who do you think you're talking to? You don't know nuthin'. Tell my baby to come home!"

With a shrug, I handed off the phone. He put it to his ear and immediately dissolved into unintelligible baby talk. I watched with parental joy as the two lovebirds reconciled. Sighing, I looked at all my check marks. *I'm so happy*, I thought, *I could just pee.*

32

Answering the Call

"**H**OW WAS YOUR NIGHT?" my wife asked as I slumped down at the kitchen table staring at a bowl of oatmeal. "See anything interesting?"

"Oh, not much," I mumbled. All I wanted was to get through my mandatory bowl of cholesterol-lowering gruel and head to bed. As I sat quietly, my mind wandered back to the night before. Actually it had been quite a night...

Around midnight, in the middle of countless patients with obscure complaints, the charge nurse handed me a chart saying, "This guy's complaining of belly pain. It doesn't sound like much. Triage got a CYA EKG by protocol. How soon can you get him out of here? We need the space."

It was true that the EKG didn't look like much. But when I began interviewing him I had a gut feeling that there was more to this one. I couldn't put my finger on it, but something didn't feel right. He kept saying that he didn't really have any chest pain. He just felt a little sick after eating a heavy meal and his wife made him come down. As I spoke to him I did something I had learned long ago; I ran my fingers across his forehead. His skin had just a touch of moisture and was slightly cool. I studied him as he spoke. The voice of experience was warning me that this guy didn't want to be sick. *This one will be subtle,* I thought. *Don't be fooled by his denials of pain.* Long nights and a few mistakes had taught me that I ignored this voice at his and my peril. So I took another, closer look at his EKG.

The computer read the EKG as normal. There were no ST elevations. But I noticed an ever so slight flattening of the ST segments in the inferior leads. "Has he received any aspirin?" I asked the nurse.

"No," she responded defensively. "He is already complaining of a sick stomach. Do you want to make him throw up?"

I ignored the wise crack and ordered dryly, "Draw the labs for a cardiac eval. If he doesn't have an aspirin allergy or an ulcer, give him some aspirin." She rolled her eyes and cocked her head as if to say, *Not another workup!* As she walked away shaking her head I felt like saying, *Don't do that. It makes your brains rattle!* I thought wiser of it, but added "And by the way, give him a milligram per kilo of Lovenox." It was the right thing to do, but I had to admit that I enjoyed saying it.

I went on with the other patients, but was soon interrupted by a holier-than-thou charge nurse. "Mr. Williams is puking his guts up," she said handing me the chart. "Now do you want to give him something to settle his aspirin-induced gastritis?"

"Sure," I said, pausing to think. "Give him some Phenergan. But would you also do another EKG." She was thoroughly put out with me now. But she was a good nurse and was only behaving this way because of the crush of patients. Within five minutes she interrupted the next patient interview to hand me the EKG.

"You better see this guy," she said, white-faced with anxiety. As I walked to the room I noticed the EKG with inferior tombstones and a noticeably slower rate.

Now he's finally showing the inferior MI that I suspected, I thought. "Get him on the pacer/monitor," I said mechanically, "in case he blocks down completely. Get a little atropine at the bedside, just for insurance. And call the cath lab to see if they want to open this guy up." I could tell that the charge nurse was embarrassed, but I ignored it. It wasn't magnanimity. This just wasn't about us. It was about saving this guy's heart.

Everyone was moving noticeably faster at the patient's bedside. He was vomiting now and starting to sweat profusely. "What's going on?" his wife demanded in the voice of near panic.

"He's having a heart attack," I said slowly, looking into her eyes. "I don't want you to worry. We have everything under control. We will either take him to the cath lab to open up his heart arteries or we'll do it with medicine." She still seemed on the verge of a meltdown. "He's pretty sick. And obviously this is very serious," I said gently putting my arm over her shoulder. "But I think there is a very good chance that he will do just fine."

"The cath lab can't do it," the clerk shouted over the nurses' station.

"OK, then we'll proceed with the thrombolysis protocol," I said to the team standing at the bedside. "I think you would do better if you waited in the waiting room," I said to the wife. But she protested and begged to remain at her husband's side. "OK," I relented, "but I need to warn you that his heart might do some funny things as the drug re-opens it. Don't be frightened. We are prepared for it."

Slowly calm was spreading in the room as everyone did their assigned jobs. And everything seemed to be going well. As the vessel opened, the STs started to come down and the patient began to report improvement. Then it happened.

Without any warning the patient suddenly went into V-tach. I grabbed the defibrillator and placed the paddles on his chest.

"Clear," I called. Pressing hard on the paddles I pushed the discharge buttons. He gave a violent leap as electricity surged through his body, to which no one in the room gave the slightest notice except for the patient's wife. She went pale. Everyone went silent as we watched the monitor. "We have normal sinus," I announced, calling off the nurse poised to start CPR.

But less then thirty seconds later the same nurse almost shouted, "We have VT again!"

"Power up to max, please," I said in a monotone. "Standby for shock." I took the paddles. "Clear." Again the patient leaped. For a moment everyone in the room studied the monitor. "We have normal sinus again," I reported. "I think we have him this time."

Only then did I notice his wife seemingly pinned to the wall. Her face was white. "Would you like to step out with me?" I asked taking her arm gently. She was shaking like a leaf in a storm.

"Pulse, pressure, and EKG have normalized," the charge said as we exited the room. "I'll get a bed in the ICU."

Everything was going to be fine with this man. Our team had worked together perfectly. But if this case was true to form we knew that we would never again hear from the patient or his wife, and the CCU and cardiologist would get the credit for saving his life.

The next patient in the rack demanded to know why it took me so long to get to her and why she couldn't see her specialist. *I don't know,* I thought. *Perhaps because he's not fool enough to stay up all hours of the night? Why do I put up with this?*

Finally, I concluded my shift with a little girl who had been crying all night with a severe earache. A bit of antibiotic, codeine, and sympathy for the exhausted mother made it seem like I was a miracle worker. "Where do you practice during normal hours?" her mother asked.

"Right here, ma'am," I chuckled. I'd received this backhanded compliment before. "This is all I do," I said. "I'm just an ER doc."

Just an ER doc? I asked myself, walking to the car after the shift. *No, I am an emergency physician.* My mind drifted back to the desert of Iraq and the words of a marine colonel. "At the end of the day," he'd said, "you can know that when a difficult job needed to be done, you answered the call." *That's right,* I almost mumbled to myself. *That's why I do this: because someone has to. Someone has to answer the call.*

"You're going to fall into that oatmeal," my wife's voice awakened me from my dreamlike memory. "And no one is on the phone. So quit telling me to answer the call. You better eat your breakfast and get to bed. You have another shift tonight."

33

Finger Pointing

THE MEDICS BURST THROUGH THE AMBULANCE entrance doors and raced to the trauma room as if some immediate action was needed to save a life. But the truth was that Wilma Jenkins's fate was sealed a split-second after the giant metal stamping machine came down and crushed both her hands.

I had taken a job doing some locums work in the small town where my aunt lived. After my mother's death, she was the only remaining relative who could tell me much about my past. So, for about a year, I traveled back and forth to this town that seemed to be in the middle of nowhere. Surrounded by farms, the townspeople were mostly truck drivers (like my aunt), unemployed, or workers at the stamping plant. The plant made a variety of things by stamping the necessary shapes into sheets of hot steel. The process took enormous sheets of steel, heated them to several thousand degrees, and then ran them through giant stampers. When a sheet had been stamped into the correct shape, an operator, like Wilma Jenkins, would reach into the stamper wearing heavy gloves and pull out the hot steel.

OSHA mandated that the machine had to be equipped with a double safety system. There was a foot pedal, a safety bar and a big red button that all had to be activated simultaneously for the stamper to work. Theoretically, all the operator's hands and feet had to be occupied doing something in the safe zone for the stamper to come crashing down with its force of several tons. However, in this case, all these safety devices had been disabled in order to allow the operator to work more quickly and produce more product.

Wilma sat stoically shaking with pain as they hurriedly moved her from the stretcher to the bed. She was still wearing the heavy gloves from work. But from the wrists down her hands looked like hapless squirrels that had been hit by a truck and run over about a thousand times. From the carpals distally her hands, including the gloves, were exactly three-eighths of an inch thick. She had apparently attempted to yank her hands out of the machine as soon as it had happened. But she had only succeeded in partially pulling off one of her hands, leaving it dangling by shreds of skin and a few loose tendons.

The nurses, normally calm, were repulsed by the sight of her hands as they started IVs in both antecubital spaces. Periodically I would catch them looking over their shoulders to catch a morbid glance of the injury. Invariably a shaking of their heads or a swearing under their collective breaths followed these glances. Everyone wanted to provide the maximum pain relief as soon as possible, but I also needed to have some reliable history. So, for a few cruel minutes, I gave her just enough morphine to take the edge off but not enough to provide total relief. Eventually we got all the information we needed and Wilma was allowed to drift away on the full effects of the drug.

"How did this happen?" I asked, confronting her supervisor on his arrival. "I thought these things were supposed to have safeties on them."

"They do!" he insisted. "She had disabled it herself."

"She did this to herself?" I stood baffled, looking at her while she slept. *How could someone be so foolish?* I began cutting off her gloves. In the process several fingers came away with the mashed material. I was flooded with a tide of emotions: pity and revulsion for her injury; frustration that I couldn't do more to help; and anger that someone was to blame for allowing this to happen.

"I know what they do out there," said the older nurse after the supervisor left the room. "They set the production quotas so high that if you want to make your bonus, you have to take off the safety bars so you can work faster. My husband used to work out there. He's seen this happen before."

"Call the orthopedic surgeon," I directed the unit clerk as I marched across the ED to encounter the supervisor. "Is this true?" I demanded after telling him what I had just learned.

"Listen, they're all adults out there," he said. "We don't tell them what to do. The machines are made with safety bars. They know they are supposed to use them."

"But is it true that you give incentives that encourage the operators to take off the safety bars?" I almost shouted as I moved closer to his face. Despite my larger size, this man was not intimidated.

"We didn't make her do what she did!" he shouted back.

"She's a single mother trying to make ends meet. And you guys barely pay above minimum wage," I said with a menacing glare.

"Listen," he said, "I've known Wilma for years. She spends over a hundred bucks a month on cigarettes and still has money to gamble on the slots at the reservation. And the truth is that if we don't increase production, this whole factory will go overseas and she won't have a job at all."

"The orthopod says he's not coming in," called out the unit clerk, further frustrating me. "He says there's nothing he can do. He said to send her to Louisville, that maybe they can salvage something or do a re-implant."

I knew that was total b.s. It was Friday night and he was at the football game. *Doesn't anyone give a damn about this poor woman?* "OK, OK," I said dejectedly. "Get the hand guy from St Agnes on the line for me. Oh, and start coordinating with the helo crew to do this transfer a.s.a.p."

After describing the injury and the preparation for transfer to the hand specialist, he asked, "Why isn't the local orthopedist handling this? It sounds like a straightforward amputation to me. What does he think I'm going to do?"

"She's got part of a finger on one hand and part of a thumb on the other. Maybe you can save them." I attempted to make the case even though I knew that both were probably not salvageable.

"And you sure don't need to waste the helo crew's time," he said ignoring me. "There's no rush on this."

I hung up the phone and gave a long sigh. I felt like leaving this town and never coming back.

Walking by the trauma room on the way to see another patient, I mentally pointed a finger at everyone that was responsible for this disaster. *If they hadn't done this, and if she hadn't done that....* It was a vicious cycle.

Then I noticed the nurse talking softly to Wilma. "It's going to be OK. Things are going to work out," she reassured the patient.

And then I saw Wilma smile. It was weak, but she definitely smiled. My jaw relaxed a bit. We hadn't been able to do much, providing a little hope and a hefty dose of morphine. But we had helped. And that was all we could do.

34

Dumbfounded

AFTER HEARING A STORY THAT BEGS for a response that one just shouldn't say, my mother-in-law has the habit of simply responding with "You don't say!" I'm sure that it's a colloquialism rooted in her determination not to say anything bad about anyone. But doctors are supposed to say something, even if it is not what the patient wants to hear. Right?

The chart said that the chief complaint was "Knee and ankle pain for one year." Besides the obvious question of 'what was it about your year-long knee and ankle pain that brought you to the ER at three in the morning,' I asked all the routine arthritis history questions. The answers were, of course, all negative. The real answer was staring me in the face. This five-foot-four patient weighed 464 pounds. When she sat on the bed her hips spread out so widely that I could set a coffee cup on the shelf they created. I paused for a moment considering the best course to take. I could prescribe a non-steroidal anti-inflammatory, like one of the prescription forms of ibuprofen. That would probably address her need for pain relief and I could move on to the next patient. But I knew that that wouldn't be addressing the real problem.

"Has anyone ever discussed with you the possibility of losing weight?" I asked gingerly.

"Not really," she said. "What's that got to do with my knees?"

"Well," I started slowly. "Carrying all that weight can be hard on your joints. Think how much your back and knees would hurt if you carried around a fifty-pound pack all day."

"You think she's got fifty pounds of fat?" her friend chimed in incredulously. I could tell that this conversation was going nowhere. Looking around at several of her friends I realized that, at six-foot-five and 230 pounds, I was a full foot taller and 150 pounds lighter than anyone in the room. I thought I'd been delicate with the suggestion of fifty pounds.

"Well," I tried again, "it could be a factor. Have you considered Weight Watchers or anything like that?"

"I had a friend who went to one of those meetings. They wouldn't let her come back because they said she broke the scales." Howls of laughter burst forth from her friends.

"You might even be a candidate for gastric bypass or banding," I said, attempting to be serious again. The whole room erupted.

"That's dangerous!"

"He don't know nuthin', baby."

"Let's go see a real doctor!"

"Maybe you could try eating Subway sandwiches?" I whimpered as the entire group started to leave the room.

"I come to the hospital with an emergency and he tells me to eat a sandwich!" the patient announced to the entire ER as she stomped by the nurses' station.

"Be sure to try some Motrin," I called to her before she got to the door.

"What was that all about?" the nurse asked. "Don't you think she has eaten enough sandwiches? You don't have to prescribe more." I could only shake my head.

Later in the night I received a toddler brought in by her mother who said that the child was a terror at home, screaming constantly.

"We let her stay up as late as she wants. She can eat anything she wants. She can watch all her favorite programs. I just don't know what's wrong with her. She must be sick or something. Could you give her something to help her sleep?" the exasperated mother pleaded.

I looked at this cute little girl, glowing in health, who simply couldn't sit still. After a benign history and physical exam I was back to the obvious. *Where do I start?* I thought. "Do you have any other children?" I asked.

The mother was struggling to control the squirming child. "She's my first, and maybe my last if I don't get something to settle her down."

It seemed clear that she was looking for some kind of medication. I was between a rock and a hard place. I could offer some practical advice on child discipline, but what could I say in fifteen minutes that would make a difference?

"Have you and your husband considered some type of counseling or parenting classes?" I posed. Then I noticed my faux pas; she wasn't wearing a wedding band.

"You think because I'm not married she needs a psychiatrist?" she asked defensively. "You think she has a mental illness?"

"No, I didn't mean that," I said. "It just might give you some tips on how to handle her."

"Oh, so you think the problem is with me and not her," she said raising her voice.

"No, no, I didn't mean that either," I said. "It's just that you might benefit from talking to someone who has been through the child rearing process. Have you talked to your mother about her behavior?"

She sat there, shaking her head in disbelief. "You're telling me to go talk to my mother? I guess if you're not going to help me..." She started picking up her things.

"I know a good book on child rearing," I offered as she reached the door. "It's called *Dare to Discipline*. It really helped us..."

"He told me to go talk to my mother," she reported disgustedly to the nurses and then left without signing anything. They looked at me with questioning stares.

"Another satisfied customer, I see," the charge nurse said. "Was that 'thunk' the sound of your Press-Ganey patient satisfaction score hitting rock bottom? You seem to have a knack for saying the wrong thing tonight." I just screwed up my face in frustration.

I finally salvaged the night when Russell came in. Everyone has a few patients like Russell. With decades of smoking more than a hundred packs a year, this scrawny veteran was not about to give up the habit. Besides, his lungs were already destroyed. His problem was both medical and mechanical. Due to the high price of tobacco, he was committed to smoking his cigarettes down to the smallest butt. And it was this that created the problem. Russell was on continuous, low-dose oxygen for his chronic lung disease. This night, as he was taking his last long drag from his cigarette, he caught his plastic oxygen cannula on fire. The flame from the burning plastic was small, but fueled by the pure oxygen. The effect was to create a tiny blowtorch right up his nose. The poor guy had second-degree burns in his nostrils. Out of pure sympathy I lobbied to the trauma surgeon for admitting him to the hospital over night. But after a full evaluation of his lung status, it was clear that the damage was superficial and he didn't need another admission. His doctor would see him in the morning.

But how was I supposed to instruct Russell before going home? After all the obvious instructions about shortness of breath and infection, what should I say about the way to prevent a reoccurrence? "Stop smoking"? That wasn't going to happen. "Stop, drop, and roll when you have a fire in your nose"?

Finally I came up with some truly practical advice that Russell might actually take. "If you must smoke, get one of those fancy cigarette holders like the old movie stars used. That way you can smoke it right to the end without getting close to your oxygen cannula."

As they rolled him out the door with a giant bandage on his nose he announced to the staff, "I'm going to look like a movie star!"

"I don't know what you told him," the charge nurse said, "but it obviously made him happy."

When I got home my wife reported that she had had an appointment with Scott, our family doctor. "He told me that my hypertension was gradually getting worse. He also said that I was in a pre-diabetic state. He made an appointment for me to see a physiatrist. I know about this guy; he has a weight loss clinic. Scott said this guy could get my hypertension and diabetes under control. I know what he's saying. He thinks I'm overweight. Sweetheart," she said while handing me a plate of my favorite waffles and bacon. "Do you think I'm fat?"

My mouth watered as I stared at the food. "He said that, huh." I picked up the biggest piece of waffle that I could possibly shove into my eager mouth. After chewing for as long as I could while my wife grew restless for an answer, I managed to mumble, "You don't say."

35

Do-It-Yourselfer

I'M PROUD OF THE FACT that I'm self-sufficient in the emergency department. It irritates the fire out of me to see prima donnas come into the department and require the entire staff to do little things they could do for themselves. I guess you could say that, during my residency, I was trained well by a charge nurse by the name of Beatrix.

Miss Bea, as she called herself, (or Miss Behemoth, as the interns called her under their breath) was a heavyset matronly type with a ruddy complexion. Her upper arms sagged and waved when she pointed to something. Though long out of style, she still wore her nursing school cap over hair that was tightly pinned and covered with a net. She once came out to the nurses' station to confront me where I was writing a note after suturing a wound. Having seen the litter of bloody gauze and needles I'd left in the room, she brought an entire roll of plaster casting material, a bucket of water, and a sling, and put it all on the counter. Deep in thought, I didn't notice her at first. But I soon heard her foot tapping and looked up to see her glaring.

"What's all this stuff for?" I asked.

"Well, I saw the mess you left," she said. "And I just assumed that both your arms were broken."

"Yes, ma'am," I said instinctively, reaching back into my childhood of groveling. "I'll clean it up, ma'am." I walked briskly to the room.

"You're damn right you'll clean it up," she lectured, following me. "Or I'll give you two broken arms."

"Yes, ma'am," I repeated several more times. The scene was reminiscent of a childhood memory where my mother made me select a branch for my own thrashing. Needless to say, the lesson in self-sufficiency took root. While the younger nurses I've worked with since are not as intimidating as Miss Bea, they can be just as stubborn.

I've had to learn how to do everything on my own. In the operating room a nurse holds up the surgical gown so that the surgeon can put his arms into it without contaminating his hands. Then, for the same reason, she holds the gloves so that he can dive his hands into them. But in the ER it's very different. I don't usually have any help. Of course, my wife has never believed this. She thinks that every time I forget to take out the trash it's because I have gotten used to an entourage of nurses picking up after me. If I ask her to hand me something she glares with a look that seems to say, *You aren't at work, Buster.* Or she'll hand me the object and say "Yes, Doctor," sarcastically adding, "Would you like me to mop your brow?" She's seen too many medical shows and thinks it's her duty to lower my expectations of stardom.

The reality is that when I'd have a minor procedure I'd set up and clean up, for the most part, by myself. I've even learned a neat trick where I have one hand wearing a sterile glove to do clean things and the other hand ungloved to touch the non-sterile objects. It's worked pretty well. Sometimes, however, attempting to fly solo has gotten me into trouble...

I knew as soon as I arrived that I would be on my own. The waiting room was full and the racks were jammed with charts. Everyone had his or her own list of tasks.

After several hours I picked up a chart with a name I recognized. Ethel Barnes was an elderly patient from a nursing home that I had seen many times before. She was morbidly obese with thinning white hair and skin to match. Unable to walk any more, she was confined to a wheel chair. And despite suffering from severe dementia, she seemed to have a jolly disposition. She just sat in her chair all day smiling and drooling. Every now and then she would make this bellowing noise, a sort of "arrrrrrgh" that sounded like Chewbacca from *Star Wars*. The clinical picture was always the same. Having had multiple abdominal surgeries over the years, her adhesions precipitated multiple episodes of mechanical bowel obstructions (in other words, severe constipation). But because of her sunny disposition, no one could tell she was in trouble until her abdomen became severely distended and uncomfortable. That's when the bellowing became louder and more frequent.

It was the same story tonight. The nursing home sheet just said "No stool for one week." *And I'm sure they just kept on feeding her,* I thought to myself.

There was no other history. The exam was predictable. The vitals were normal as was everything else except for her massive, distended, silent abdomen. She seemed oblivious to her condition. I ordered the basic labs and an abdominal series of x-rays to rule out another obstruction, and then dashed off to the next patient.

About an hour later her chart resurfaced. The labs were all normal. The x-rays, too, were unremarkable, except for the huge amount of stool present in her colon. I returned to the room to make a final check before sending her back to the nursing home. *They can clean out her gut just as easily as we can,* I mused. But when I opened the door I found Ethel sitting in a wheelchair beside her bed surrounded by a pool of diarrhea. Apparently she had only had a stool plug in her rectum. Everything behind it was liquid. Once the plug had dislodged, she had emptied her entire bowel. It had overflowed her diaper, filled her seat, run down her legs and formed a large brown puddle around her wheelchair. She sat there grinning.

"Ethel, Ethel...what am I going to do with you?" I asked aloud. "Well, first we have to get you out of that soiled hospital gown."

By stretching my legs as far as they would go I was able to straddle the puddle and reach her neck to untie the soiled gown. Pitching it to the side, I then unwisely decided to attempt the one-man, move-the-fat-lady-to-the-stretcher maneuver. Facing her, I reached under her armpits and embraced her in a giant bear hug, then lifted with all my might. Once I had raised her massive hips from the chair I quickly kicked the wheelchair out of the way. My plan was to take one large step over the puddle and muscle her onto the clean bed. And it was working until her sagging buttocks hit the unlocked bed, sending it rolling across the room. Now I was stuck with her, suspended over the muck.

I studied the problem for a brief moment, but noticed that one of my feet was beginning to slide ever so slowly. It turned out that when my chair-kicking foot landed, it was right on the edge of the puddle of liquid stool. I tried several times to regain my footing without stepping into the middle of the puddle, but nothing would stop our relentless slide to the floor. Wishing to save my hands from complete contamination, I pulled out and placed them on her shoulders. When we finally came to rest, I was spread-eagled over an obese, senile, naked lady in a pool of diarrhea.

"Help," I called out softly, not wishing to draw too much attention. "Help," again, somewhat louder. Finally in full voice, "I need some help in here!"

"Doctor Plaster is calling for help in room twelve!" I heard someone shout. *Oh no*, I thought. *They think it's a code.*

The door flew open and the charge nurse just stood there. "What are you doing?" she deadpanned after a long pause.

"I was sailing on the Shit Sea and got marooned on Blubber Island!" I yelled. "What do you think I was doing? Help me get off of her." Ethel smiled, drooled, and gave a loud "Arrgggh!"

As expected everyone came running up with the crash cart, saw what was going on, and then began snickering. With help I was able to climb off of

Ethel. But I had to immediately change into a set of scrubs and bag my clothing. Housekeeping cleaned up the mess in the room and a nurse's aide got tagged to clean up Ethel. Afterward the nurses continued with a relentless banter of sailing jokes. I couldn't wait to head home.

"How was your night?" my wife asked in her usual fashion as I returned from the laundry room after dumping my clothes in the wash.

"You don't even want to know," I said with a look that warned her not to pursue the issue.

"OK," she said slowly. "Well, then, on another note. The toilet's not working again."

"Oh, I can fix that," I said reflexively. "The plumber always charges an arm and a leg. I'll do it."

"You are going to fix the toilet by yourself?" she asked. "You?"

Our eyes met in a long question. "You know," I finally said. "On second thought, I think I'll let him handle it. He has a helper."

36

Geezer

I SAT NERVOUSLY IN THE ED DIRECTOR'S OFFICE as he went through the required chart review. Mike was extremely courteous and respectful while pointing out some obvious deficiencies and other areas of possible improvement in my practice. I tried to diffuse my anxiety by commenting on a birthday card on his desk.

"Yeah, I'm the big four-oh," he said with a slight sigh of resignation.

"Hey, you're still a baby," I kidded.

"Oh, I know," he smirked. "I just hope I'm still able to do night shifts when I'm your age."

My age? MY AGE? His comment exploded in my atrophied brain while I tried to keep my face as blank as a Botox OD.

"And by the way," he continued, "I want you to know that you're a real inspiration to us younger guys. The way you've continued to do clinical shifts as you've gotten older..."

By the time I got home from my shift my oral mucosa was all dried out from shuffling around all night with my mouth open.

"Can you believe he said that?" I said indignantly to my wife the next morning as I was shoveling in the oatmeal.

"Honey, I'm sure he meant it as a sincere compliment."

"Hey," I shot back, "I've still got a lot more hair than he does."

My college-aged daughter swept into the kitchen and chimed in. "Yeah Pop, but you can't count all the hair in your ears and nose." She giggled and grabbed a banana off the table.

"Hey, young lady," I glared. "Don't call me 'Pop.' That's saved for the grandbabies."

"I'm your daughter, aren't I?" she said.

"Not for long, if you keep this up."

"Oh, honorable father," she smiled. "Confucius say, not wise to criticize another man's roof when your own roof show signs of wear."

"She's right, sweetheart," my wife said. "Have you looked at the back of your head recently?"

Instinctively I reached for the top of my head and felt flushed skin. "Well, this isn't about hair, anyway," I said, shaking my head. "It's about whether ER docs get better as they get older. Heck, if you needed hair to be smart, Rick Bukata would have retired a long time ago."

"I know one ER doc who's getting better as he gets older," my wife said with her favorite come-hither look.

"That's right, baby," I shouted boisterously. I jumped up to my body builder pose. "ER docs do it all night!" I tried to slap her behind as she walked by.

"Oh my gosh," my daughter said screwing up her face. "I hate it when you guys do that geezer sex talk thing."

"Geezer? I think it's time for you to go back to college, young lady. Leave your mother and me alone in the house for a weekend."

"Speaking of weekends," my wife joined, "don't you think it's time you cut back on some of your shifts? Maybe you could give some of them over to Nilantha."

"What's Nilantha?" my daughter jumped back in.

"Not what. Who," I said. "He's one of my new partners. He just graduated from residency. His name is Sri Lankan for 'My kid's a lot smarter than your kid.' You know these guys coming out of residency are so smart these days. I don't think I could get into an emergency medicine residency today."

"He's getting married soon," my wife said. "And his fiancée has invited 800 relatives. I'm sure he could use the additional money." I could see where she was headed and she was pushing her advantage.

"But I'm not too old to do this," I insisted. "I saw Greg Henry at ACEP last month and he said he was going to keep going until they had to push him around in a wheelchair. And did you see Jerry Hoffman? He looks like Father Time! They're both still doing it."

"I think they are mostly lecturing," she responded rather pedantically. "No longer working weekend nights. It's hard on your body."

"I'm still strong," I bragged without convincing anyone, least of all myself.

"Hey, dad," my daughter said. "I know you have your annual physical fitness test coming up for the navy. Do you want to go out running with me today?"

"Sure," I said. "How far do you plan to run?"

"Only five today," she said. "I'll take it easy on you."

"Is that five blocks or five kilometers?" I asked with a growing queasiness in my stomach.

"Uh, five miles," she came back.

I knew that if I took the bait I would be in rigor mortis in about five hours. "Hey, let me take a rain check on that. My knee's been bothering me at work lately."

"See, that's what I mean," my wife said. "You need to take it a little easier."

I felt caught between the two women in my life. "But I like it," I whined.

"No you don't," my wife said. "I hear you complaining about it all the time."

"I need the money," I whined again.

"No you don't," she said again.

"It's part of who I am," I finally said.

She had no other play. "Will you at least *consider* cutting back?"

"OK," I finally conceded. I stumbled off to bed but slept fitfully. My dreams alternated between running the Marine Corps Marathon and getting shuffled off to a nursing home. I awakened exhausted. Grumpy and tired I headed off to work without another word to my wife or daughter.

As I rushed from patient to patient I was trying to practice perfectly. It's not necessarily that I had something to prove, I just wanted to do good work. But one of the patients really caught my attention. While doing the history and physical, I noticed two important things. First, he looked like hell; he had, as my mother used to say, one foot in the grave and the other on a banana peel. And second, we shared the same birth year. I examined him closely, but my mind was doing a little comparative anatomy as well. After leaving the exam room I confronted his nurse.

"Hey, Michele," I said. "Does that guy look the same age as me?"

"Heck, no!" she said with enthusiasm. "He's got to be at least twenty years older than you."

I always liked working with Michele. I think she's one of the smartest nurses I've ever worked with.

37

Hero

IT WAS SATURDAY NIGHT OF VETERANS DAY weekend. I arrived for the night shift in a mood to save the world from death and disease. As I ran the board with Andy, the doc who I was relieving, he suddenly stopped. "See that guy in triage? If he comes in once more with bumps on his penis, just kick him out. I've seen him nine times for that. It's nothing. I think he just likes to expose himself."

"It's too late," the PA said. "I've already seen him in Fast Track. I didn't see any bumps either, but I gave him some Zovirax ointment."

"Did you think it was herpetic?" I asked seriously.

"No," she shrugged.

"Tell him to use Vaseline. It'll do the same thing and it's cheaper," Andy said heading for the door.

This was not exactly what I had in mind when I went into emergency medicine. Funny penile bumps being treated with placebo ointments. *Hopefully,* I thought, *the night will get better.* It didn't.

The first room held an elderly man with an emesis basin full of yellow vomitus. "I have cancer," he said blankly after I introduced myself. "It's spread all over. They thought they had it but now it's back. The chemo makes me sick. Oh, and I've been passing blood, too."

"Really? Does your oncologist know about this?" I inquired.

"Yeah," he grimaced. "He doesn't care."

I was sure he would be an admission and started the workup. "Don't worry," I reassured him. "We'll get you fixed up." During the exam I noticed a long abdominal scar. "What's this from?" I quizzed.

"Gun shot wound," he said enigmatically.

"Oh...how'd it happen?" I was eager with the anticipation of hearing a great World War II story.

"You don't need to know," he said looking away.

Despite this man's benign appearance, I came to suspect that he probably had a dark past. For whatever reason, he was facing the end of his life without the apparent support of a single friend or family member.

I tried to stop his nausea but nothing helped. I called his oncologist. He knew everything about the old man, and didn't want to admit him unless there was an obstruction. Which there wasn't. The labs were fine. After the workup I attempted to call back the oncologist to plead the case for a respite admission. But after several unanswered attempts I gave up. In truth, the patient really didn't need a medical admission. He just needed someone to give a damn.

"Feeling better?" I asked, poking my head in the door.

"Not really," he said. "But I think I'll go home now."

"Are you sure? You can stay here a while. We'll try other things."

"Hey doc," he said, seeming to sense my frustration. "I know you tried. And I really appreciate that." I appreciated him letting me off the hook; but in truth, he was a total treatment failure. He left barely any better than when he arrived.

The next case was simple, an eighteen-month-old boy with wheezing. He'd had a low-grade fever the day before, but now he only had a slight wheeze, barely audible in the quiet room. He was a cute little guy who played with my flashlight throughout the exam. Actually he was fine. But his mother was obviously very concerned. She sat tensely beside the bed as if counting his breaths. I knew it was likely to be garden-variety viral bronchiolitis, possibly RSV, and told the mother so. The baby obviously didn't need hospitalization, and I suspected therapy would do little good. Nevertheless, I ordered a chest x-ray, an RSV swab and a neb, hoping to find a way to treat the wheeze for his mother's sake. But nothing helped. I was striking out.

At the recheck I assured the mom that, despite the unchanged condition, her little boy would do fine.

"Are you sure?" she almost pleaded.

"I'm sure," I said, instinctively reaching to touch her hand. The mother's countenance visibly changed. It was clear that she felt better, but I sure didn't.

The rest of the night was more of the same. Cases consisted of problems that were either unfixable or not problems at all. By the time I got home, I was frustrated and restless despite my fatigue.

"Better get dressed for church," my wife breezed through the kitchen where I was stirring my oatmeal. "Remember, this is Veterans Day weekend. I had your dress blues cleaned. They are going to be honoring all the service men and women. And speaking of my favorite hero, who did you help save last night?"

"Nobody," I mumbled.

"You got a letter from the hospital vice president," she said catching my attention. "He told me someone wrote in to say that you were very empathetic. That's nice."

"That's me all right," I responded. "Dr. M. Pathetic." My wife's look was a scolding question. "Hey, I'm an emergency physician. I cut open chests and restart hearts. I reassemble shattered faces. Who did our son tell everyone at school was his hero? Me. I'm the guy who can raise the dead, remember? But last night all I did was hold hands and hug babies." I sighed. "Sometimes that just doesn't do it for me..." She simply shook her head and walked away.

As we approached the Naval Academy chapel, several people stopped those of us in uniform to express their gratitude for our service. I politely nodded to acknowledge their comments but remained in something of a funk. Later I sat in the pew half dosing and half reevaluating my professional motivation.

"Knowledge will pass," I heard the chaplain say. "But love never fails."

I looked at my wife just as she looked at me. "The last word in health care," she mouthed, parroting a cliché that she'd heard me say before. She was right and I knew that. But sometimes I hated to admit she was right.

Reading further, the chaplain continued. "When I was a child I thought like a child, but when I became a man I put away childish things..." My wife looked at me again, pointing at me with her eyebrows.

"OK, OK," I whispered. "I get it. Stop looking at me like that."

38

Homicide

IT WAS A HOT AUGUST NIGHT, so getting a call that the medics were bringing in a "gunshot to the head" wasn't much of a surprise. It's a proven axiom of emergency medicine that the incidence of penetrating trauma rises with the mercury. We were still preparing for their arrival when two sweating medics came through the ambulance doors towing a huge man on their gurney. It was clear that this was a scoop and run because they had not even attempted an IV. The trailing medic was working at bagging the patient, trying to assist breathing with a facemask and a bag/valve/mask device. But as he approached the trauma room he gave up and threw the Ambu bag onto the patient's chest.

"Don't waste your time with this guy," the lead medic said. "He's got a .38 caliber entrance behind his right ear and no exit. He had a little pulse when we got there, but it seems to be fading fast."

I stood idly in the corner while the medics hoisted the big man roughly over to the ER cart. He was built like an NFL lineman, with tattoos all over his neck, chest and arms. But the truly remarkable feature was the look on his face. Apparently the shockwave from the bullet to the head had caused the tissues behind his eyes to swell, pushing his eyeballs forward. This gave him the appearance of a wide-eyed expression.

"Hey doc," said the medic. "See his face? Looks like he's saying 'What the f—'"

"Let's see if we can at least preserve his organs for possible transplantation," I interrupted the medic as the trauma team began opening the trauma trays.

"I don't think you want to do that." The voice came from a cop who had just walked into the room. "He was recently incarcerated for a drug charge. He's probably got HIV. Besides we'll have to do a full criminal investigation."

I went ahead with my preparation to tube the guy. "Do you know who shot him?" I asked.

"Yeah," he replied. "I did."

I stopped and faced the policeman. "You shot this guy? In the back of the head?"

"Yeah," he said with a little attitude. "He was about to stab his ole lady."

"We've totally lost his pulse," the charge nurse said. "And he's completely apneic. Are you sure you want to code this guy?"

I looked around the room at everyone standing passively. "I guess not," I said. "For the record, death was pronounced at 02:34." The trauma recorder began writing and everyone else started cleaning the room. I turned back to the cop. "Are you going to get in a lot of trouble for shooting this guy like this?"

"It's not like that," he said defensively. "This bum is a known abuser. We've been over to that place a million times. His ole lady had finally had enough and pressed charges. She got the restraining order. But this idiot, the first thing he did when he got out of jail was to go over and try to tap dance on her head again."

"Guys like him ought to be castrated," hissed Debbie who did all the SANE (Sexual Assault Nurse Examiner) exams.

"Men are scum. I wish someone would've shot my ex," mumbled Tracy who was married to her third fireman.

"Whoa, ladies. Back away from the knives and guns," I taunted. "Don't start nuking the whole male gender. Maybe he was abused by his mother when he was little." At that every woman in the room stopped to look at me. I made an effort to conciliate. "Hey, all I'm saying is that he might deserve the benefit of the doubt." Turning to the cop, I attempted to change the subject. "So you're not going to get in trouble for shooting a guy like this?" The powder burns on the back of the victim's head indicated that the policeman had fired his gun from only inches away.

"I don't think so," he said defiantly. "He busted through the door and chased her to the neighbor's house. When he heard her calling the police he busted through the neighbor's door. He had her on the floor when we arrived."

"Did you try to reason with him? Did you even try to talk him down?"

"Listen, doc!" I could hear the frustration in his voice. "His ole lady had tried turning the other cheek. And every time he just hit her harder. Like I said, he had her on the floor, beating her when we arrived. I yelled 'police.' He reached for the knife. I shot him. That's all there is to it."

"And you didn't try to take the knife away from him?" Apparently I had stepped over the line. Despite the cop's smaller stature he walked over to face me.

"Have you ever been in a fight?" he asked calmly.

"Not really," I said, somewhat intimidated.

"Well, if a man like that has a knife, you don't fight him in a dark room," the cop said. "There's no telling what will happen."

I took a deep breath, looking back at the naked man on the table with his huge muscles and bug-eyed expression. "You're right," I sighed. I guess I understood. But I was still having a hard time getting my head around the fact that the person in front of me had killed another human being in that way. "I can't imagine having your job," I said. "Won't you have nightmares of what just happened? What did you feel when you shot him?"

"Oh, a little recoil from my weapon. But not much," he joked, finally lightening up. "Hey Doc, you've been watching too many cop shows. I'm going to fill out the paperwork for the investigation. Then when I get off the shift I'm going to have a steak and eggs…and a beer."

"Is his girlfriend going to be OK?" I was actually wondering whether I was going to be receiving the other half of this incident.

"Oh, she was a little shook up at the scene. But she feels better now," he added with a smile. "You want to know why? She knows she won't be getting any more beatings."

39

Just Keeping Up

IT LOOKED LIKE IT WAS GOING TO BE a slow night as I made my way from the parking lot to the ambulance entrance. The patient parking lot was only half full. The weather was clear and unseasonably warm. I was whistling a happy tune. But the inside of the ED was another story. Every room was full and there were nine charts in the 'To Be Seen' rack. And the computer had the names of at least nine more waiting to get into the ED. The two doctors on day shift were definitely not slackers. They had just gotten overrun.

I thumbed through the complaints in the rack. 'Belly pain,' 'belly pain,' 'shoulder pain,' 'intoxicated and fell,' and another 'belly pain.' *What's going on? This can't be carryover from Thanksgiving.* Then I noticed that many of the patients were wearing purple, the team color of the Baltimore Ravens. *They're all coming from the stadium. They've all been eating junk food, drinking beer after beer, and falling down the stadium steps.* Our group ran the stadium clinic, so many of these people were being shuttled over from the game. They were actually coming by the proverbial busloads.

My first patient of the evening was an obese woman wearing the jersey of her favorite offensive tackle. Additionally she had purple lipstick, purple fingernails, purple ear bangles, and purple hair. When I complimented her team spirit she quickly lifted her jersey to show me her purple bra. She offered to show off her purple thong but I declined as gracefully as I could. The thought of Barney in a thong made me feel queasy. She had eaten at least six hot dogs and drunk as many beers and was wondering why her gall bladder was bothering her.

The next chart I picked up had the complaint of syncope. *Fainting*, I thought, *might be a little more interesting*. But no, she was also a drunk fan. Halfway through the exam she began wailing, "I never drink!"

"Don't worry," I deadpanned. "You'll be fine by tomorrow."

"I'm a first grade teacher at a Catholic school. I'm going to lose my job for this," she blubbered.

I opened the chart to see that her alcohol level was two-and-a-half times the legal driving limit. Just then she sat up and hurled a large volume of partially digested nachos into her own lap.

"OK, maybe you can take tomorrow off," I said, moving quickly out of the line of fire.

Looking at the bright side of this madness, these were all paying patients. And after today's big football win, my Press-Ganey scores might get a little bump, if they could remember that they were here.

Then I got a reality check. "Gunshot wound to the right chest. Thirteen-year-old male. No vitals. ETA three minutes," I heard the radio crackle. I moved quickly to the trauma room but my partner was already there calmly directing everyone as they prepared to receive the patient. The truth was that I was not needed. But I was captivated by the adrenaline of the situation. I told myself that I would be helping.

The patient looked much older than thirteen. Already too experienced in the world of the nearby project, he had a large tattoo on his arm. He had apparently attempted to fend off a spray of high caliber bullets shot at close range. One bullet had passed through his right wrist shattering the radius before entering his chest and traversing the mediastinum. Raising his arm to prepare for the chest tube made his hand flop like he was waving goodbye. Everyone jumped in to place the ET tube, chest tubes, central lines, NG tube, Foley, and blood draws, all while performing continuous CPR. But throughout the code the monitor showed only wide complexes of agonal PEA.

"How long has he been down?" I finally asked the medic.

"As long as twenty minutes before we arrived," he answered. The air seemed to be sucked out of the room. The once energetic code became coldly efficient in recognition of the fact that a cardiac save would probably be a neurological disaster. Nevertheless, the trauma team leader made every effort before calling the code. As he began wrapping up the paperwork I returned to the ED, which by now resembled O'Hare International Airport...in a snowstorm. The evening shift doctor tried his best to help me catch up before he left, even working several hours after his twelve-hour shift had ended. But my fate for the night was already set.

About three in the morning the nurses realized that we were so backed up we were nearing a diversion point. I knew if we went on diversion that within an hour other hospitals would go as well and ambulances would be caught in gridlock. We would fight hard not to go on diversion.

"Doctor Sylvester's on line twelve," the unit clerk announced.

"Did we call you?" I asked the ED director, somewhat bewildered.

"No," he slurred, obviously half asleep. "The nurses called to see if I could come in to give you some help." I felt like a kid who was caught without his homework done. I'm the guy who can always move patients. What were they doing waking up the director to drag him in here to help me? "Don't worry, they're supposed to call," he said calmly trying to reassure me. He could hear the embarrassment in my voice.

"No, no, no," I said quickly. "We're fine. I just got a little backed up with a shooting earlier in the evening. I'm catching up now." I thought that would end the conversation.

"The nurses told me about that. They said it tied up both doctors for over an hour." I knew where this was going. "Did the case really need both of you?" From some people that could have sounded callous and uncaring, but I knew Hank. He always had the patients' interests at heart, all the patients. It might have been easier to ignore if I'd thought he was just yanking my chain, doing the ED director thing. But he wasn't.

"No," I confessed. In my head I could hear myself chastising my navy corpsmen. "The hardest decisions in emergency medicine are when you have to cut your losses on people that you can't save and move on to people that you can." I told them of corpsmen who had either been killed or let someone else die while they used all their resources on a case they knew was not savable from the start. Resuscitation takes precious time and resources, and it should not be wasted.

"Do you need me to come in?" he asked. I knew he meant it honestly and wasn't just testing me.

"No," I said firmly. "All the complaints that are waiting are minor. By the time you get here I'll have them cleaned up." It was a half-truth. Hidden among all the minor complaints were some truly sick patients that had waited for hours. Several had to be admitted and there were more in the waiting room.

The rest of the morning I raced from room to room, apologizing to everyone for the delays and thanking them for their patience. By the time my shift was ending, my only consolation was that I had gotten the "To Be Seen" rack back to the place where it had been when I arrived.

Arriving home I was confronted by my wife's usual cheery "How'd your night go, honey?" I sat dumbly at the breakfast table drinking in the peace. The contrast was like racing into warmth after taking the Polar Bear Plunge.

"Pretty well, I guess," I sighed. "I saved a first-grade teacher from getting fired. And it was a close call but I think I saved myself from a lifetime of Barney nightmares." She peered at me quizzically. "But I lost a thirteen-year-old to terminal social necrosis." My wife looked at me like I was speaking Swahili. "I guess I did OK. I kept up. Oh, and the Ravens won."

40

One at a Time

I COULD SEE THE MAN'S FACE TURN PALE as I slid into the middle seat beside him. I'm six feet, five inches tall with an equal wingspan and weigh two hundred and forty pounds. And we were on our way to Nairobi...from Detroit. He looked at me like we were on our way to Hell. He immediately submerged himself into an expensive headset and tried to ignore me. I tried to respect what little privacy he had, but my innate curiosity finally prevailed and so I struck up a conversation over our box dinner.

He was German. And once I got past the cultural aloofness that he projected I discovered a warm and engaging personality. He had spent his entire career working in Africa with NGOs, non-governmental aid organizations. He was on his way to the Democratic Republic of the Congo, formerly Zaire. "That's where the International Criminal Court is trying that general for using child soldiers," I said, attempting to show that Americans do know about world affairs. "What's that all about?" I asked.

"They go into villages and force the little boys to rape and murder their parents. Then, when the boys can never return to their homes, they assimilate them into the army," he explained.

I was on business with the Marine Corps so it was easy to compare these "soldiers" to the battle-hardened troops that I'd worked with in combat situations. I couldn't imagine an army of children. "What good is it to have a military made up of little boys?" I asked shaking my head.

"Oh, you don't understand," he went on. "These little boys are killing machines. They are completely antisocial and amoral. The army is their only family. They don't seem to have any moral conception of suffering and death. I recently had a confrontation with one of these 'soldiers,'" he recalled with cold detachment. "He was smoking a joint, had a bottle of whisky in one hand, and was pointing a Kalashnikov rifle at me. The look in his eye was completely devoid of humanity." Then he added chillingly, "If I could have, I would have killed him on the spot."

"Do you have children?" I asked after a long silence, trying to lighten the mood.

"Yes, they are back in Germany with my wife," he answered with a distant smile. "After my wife and children were taken hostage by rebels for three days, we decided that the family should go back to Germany to stay."

I sat in stunned silence.

"I'm amazed that you are returning. You must care deeply for the people of the Congo." I felt honored to have met such a man. Then he shocked me again.

"I don't give a damn about the people of the Congo anymore," he said bluntly. "It's just how I make a living. I enjoy traveling and learning new languages. This job allows me the opportunity to do both."

Two weeks later I was back in the emergency department at home. Hippos, zebras, and mud huts were a distant and fading memory. But as I trudged from room to room with my arms full of charts I couldn't shake the picture of that little boy soldier and the cynical aid worker. Somehow life had robbed both of them, the child of his innocence and the man of his idealism. This was the global war that gave terrorism its face. *Can a kid like that ever be saved?* I asked myself. The question seemed to hang over me like the relentless equatorial sun.

As I entered the room to see my first patient of the night I had to stifle a laugh. The heavily muscled man sitting in the chair looked like a WWF wrestler wannabe. His hair was cut in a mullet and he sported a big gold ring in one earlobe. He was wearing a Harley-Davidson t-shirt that was cut at the shoulders to allow room for his massive biceps and triceps.

But he wasn't the one who made me smile. Sitting beside him was a skinny little boy with a frightened look on his face wearing the exact same garb. He had the same mullet hair, oversized earring, and cut-off Harley shirt. The only major difference was that his frame was so small that the t-shirt bagged loosely about his thin arms and chest. The Band-Aid on his chin told me that he was the patient and that his motorcycle-riding father was here to make sure everything went well.

The little boy's injury was the usual laceration to the chin. As I explained the repair procedure to the father he never blinked or took his eyes off me. And the little boy never took his eyes off his dad. When the nurse came into the room carrying a large papoose-type restraint, the father said in a deep raspy voice, "You won't need that." After tenderly laying the boy on the bed, he spoke to him firmly. "Now lay still and let the doctor fix you up." Despite my best efforts to hide the size of the lidocaine injector, the boy saw it, shot a look at his father, and went stiff as a board. "It'll be OK. I promise," the man croaked. "Right, Doc?"

"It'll sting a little, but you can take it," I said. The little boy tightened and stifled a cry with each burn of the needle. The father was reaching across his son's chest holding the boy's arms. But I soon realized it was more reassurance than restraint. His face was near the boy's chin and I could see him wince each time I pierced the boy's skin with the needle. One time I even caught the man attempting to hide a tear by putting his face into the boy's chest. When it was finally over he stood up to stretch his back and reached out to take his son. The boy literally leaped into the big man's arms.

"Would you like to pick out some stickers?" the nurse asked as she handed the father the home-going instructions.

The boy turned to his dad. "Can I have more than one?"

"Just leave a few for the other kids," he growled. He seemed like a friendly bear.

"You are really good with your son," I said. "He obviously looks up to you."

"Oh, he's not my kid," the man rasped.

"Really?" I asked.

"He's just a stray from the neighborhood. I don't know if his ole man has ever been in the picture. And his mother is high most the time. The boy comes over to our house to get away from his mother's boyfriends. We do our best to love and protect him."

"Really," I said smiling. I paused to study the man. He wasn't the person I'd assumed he was. "I admire what you're doing for that little boy."

He looked at me quizzically. "It's not like I'm saving the world, like you are, Doc," he said with a shrug.

"Oh, but you are," I said.

41

Therapy Session

IT WAS THE LAST NIGHT in my off-work cycle before embarking on a long string of night shifts. My wife and I had planned to have a nice dinner. Maybe watch a movie. And head to bed early. So it was not a particularly good time to get into a fight with her. But I've never been known for great timing. I don't even remember what it was all about. I only recall that an annoyance was met with a sarcasm that resulted in a downward spiral of accusations, rationalizations, more accusations, and finally dredged-up hurts from past years. It was stupid and ugly.

"I think I'm going to sleep in the guest room," my wife said with tears in her eyes.

"I think I'll go sleep in a motel," I countered, proving once and for all that doctoral degrees have been awarded to complete morons. As I stomped out to the car I realized that I had no intention of going to a motel. *I'll just do like they do in the movies,* I thought. *I'll go to the nearest tavern and make my case before the bartender. I'm sure he'll understand and support me.*

I went to a place around the corner expecting to see some wizened old guy named Joe in a white shirt, bowtie, and apron. Instead, behind the bar was a six-foot-four, three-hundred-pound woman with dyed black hair, a tattoo and scowl to match, who looked like she'd just stepped out of the roller derby. It was late and there was only one old couple looking like they were ready to go home. It was clear the bartender wanted to close and was in no mood for small talk, let alone affirmation.

I sat there in depressed silence nursing a beer while staring at some stupid quiz game on the TV screen. *How can I be such an idiot?* I sighed to myself. *It's easy. You've been doing it for years, my conscience answered.* Finally my better self started to get the upper hand. *Maybe if I get home quick enough I can at least salvage part of the evening...* I slapped down some money on the bar with determined repentance and walked quickly to the car. Creeping into the house and peering in the guest room I discovered I was too late. My wife was already soundly asleep.

Slipping into bed with her without gaining her forgiveness was too presumptuous. Sleeping alone in our bed seemed hardhearted and arrogant. So the only alternative was the couch. But I soon remembered why I never napped on the couch; it was too short. If I laid my head on the armrest I got a crick in my neck. If I put my feet on the other armrest my knees ached and my legs went to sleep. I did finally doze off. But by morning I was a drooling mass of aches and pains. And my wife was gone, presumably avoiding me. I tried to get in touch with her before leaving for work, but to no avail. I arrived at the hospital fatigued with sore knees and a heavy heart.

Around midnight I picked up a chart with a chief complaint that read "Suicidal ideation." The patient was a man in his thirties, immaculately dressed, with an expensive gold watch and bracelet. His shirt was unbuttoned just so in a seeming attempt at machismo.

"I'm depressed, Doc," he said immediately after our introductions.

"I know how you feel," I sighed, thinking about the night before.

"I think I need to be admitted to the hospital for a few days," he went on. "I've been thinking a lot about suicide." I knew our recently renovated psych facility was pretty nice, but he talked about it like he was checking into a resort spa. And he emphasized the "S" word like it was his MasterCard.

Therapy Session

"Really?" I questioned. "Why would you want to do that?"

"I don't think my wife loves me anymore," he said starting to whine a little.

"OK...I hear you." It wasn't hard to commiserate a little with him. "What did you do?"

"Oh, it's not me," he snapped. "It's her. She doesn't affirm me like I need. When we met she fell madly in love with me. I was a dashing young executive and she was just a secretary." *Did he really just say 'dashing?'* He continued to sink into self-absorption. "She doesn't appreciate how I elevated her status. Oh, at first she did. But now she just sort of ignores me."

"Did she start seeing someone else?" I asked.

"She would never cheat on me," he said coldly. "I lost interest in her."

I was starting to see the picture. "And you started stepping out."

"Of course, a few times. Other women find me attractive."

"Which came first, the loss of 'affirmation' or the affairs?" I asked rhetorically, hoping he would see the connection.

"She just wasn't meeting my needs anymore. She was really destroying my self-esteem," he answered.

"Oh, so you left her?"

"Well, actually she kicked me out. Now I don't have anywhere to go."

"I thought you were the executive?"

"The sports car is mine, but she owns the condo." He was rapidly losing my sympathy. This was starting to look more like a search for three hots and a cot. I just needed to document the true risk to the patient.

"How's your appetite? Would you like me to get you a sandwich?"

"A burger would be great," he said. I was actually thinking of a tuna sandwich from the vending machine.

"How have you been sleeping? How about your sex life?" I was checking off the 'No' boxes on the suicide checklist.

"Great, until my girlfriend started seeing someone else."

"Who wasn't 'firming enough, her or you?" I punned. But he missed it.

"Have you felt like giving away any of your possessions? You know, have you considered giving your car to a charity?"

"No," he said indignantly.

"Have you thought about how you would kill yourself? Have you thought of taking poison? I had a guy once who drank two whole cans of Drano. At surgery his gut was dead from mouth to anus. He didn't make it." I saw the color drain from his face. "Or maybe you've thought of shooting yourself. Do you have any guns in the house? I once had a guy who was depressed and wanted to shoot himself. The only problem was he used a shotgun and since he was a little guy like you he couldn't quite reach the trigger. So the air column from the barrel forced his head back and he only blew off his face." I saw his jaw literally drop and he looked like he was going to vomit. "Actually he felt better after we kind of put his face back together. Have you ever been tempted to do something like that?"

"No!" he almost shouted. Swallowing hard, he tried to regain his composure. "You know, Doc, you're really crazy."

"No, I'm not," I said writing on the chart. "And neither are you. You should consider your low self-esteem as just good common sense. Hospitalization will not help you. The best thing for you to do is to go back to your wife, get on your knees, admit you've been a jerk, and ask for her forgiveness. Maybe she'll take you back." He was not a happy camper as I left the room, but I felt a lot better.

Driving home after the shift I was tasting my words and preparing my speech of contrition. So I was surprised to see my wife sitting on the front steps with two cups of coffee.

"I can be really stupid," I blurted. "Can you find it in your heart to forgive me?"

"Before you even asked," she said, handing me a cup and patting the step beside her. "How was your night at the Super 8?"

42

Wedding Bell Blues

IT WAS THE KIND OF HOT DAY in the city where people had been sitting on the stoops of their row homes, drinking beers, and arguing with passersby. So in the ED there was a lot of minor trauma mixed in with a few big cases. Consequently I didn't read any further than "Altercation" in the chief complaint on the top chart of the stack that I was carrying. But when I entered the room it was obvious that I had missed something.

The patient was a young woman in her mid twenties who appeared somewhat older, even matronly because of her size and dress. She had not bothered to undress and was still wearing a cream-colored silk business suit, complete with matching hat, gloves, and high heels. I say matronly not because of that softness of a mother, but because it appeared that she had already put on her middle-age spread. The sheer girth of the woman was stressing the seams of her straight skirt to the max. But she wasn't fat; she was just big. This was not a woman to mess with.

As I introduced myself she just laid on the bed holding her matching purse with both hands while staring off with a look of triumphant resolution. Her injuries were as many as they were minor. She had a swollen right eye, a split lip, scratches on her face, and abrasions to both knees. The blouse that had been tied at the neck was torn and open where someone had obviously attempted to drag or strangle her with it. However, it appeared that she had inflicted a little damage herself. Both hands exhibited signs of having delivered more than a few solid blows. Her gloves were torn and dirty, and her knuckles demonstrated the unmistakable marks of someone's teeth.

"Where did this happen?" I asked after assessing the damage.

"At church," she said without looking at me. Her chin seemed to rise a bit as she recalled the incident.

"Did someone try to rob you as you were going to church?" I was guessing now.

"No," she said, making eye contact for the first time. Now I was really curious. I hated it when that happened. The injuries were minor and the details of the history had no real bearing on what kind of medical care I was going to render. It was none of my business, but I just wanted to know.

Like the eighty-year-old guy who came in one time with a Christmas tree-shaped lightbulb in his rectum. Any reasonable person would want to know, just like I did, "What the heck were you thinking when you shoved that up there? That this is the season to be jolly, so I'll just light up my back side?" Maybe a reasonable person wouldn't be so bold or presumptuous. Maybe one would have just said, "Dude, that must really hurt." The real problem in asking needless questions is that they often lead to other needless questions. As in this case, the old man told me his doctor suggested the light bulb as a treatment for his hemorrhoids. He said he'd been doing it for years and it had always worked before. Of course this response brought up a whole new set of questions. Like, "Do I look so stupid that I would believe a story like that?" Or, "What country is this that a licensed physician would prescribe a light bulb in the butt to treat anything?"

Anyway, despite my mind warning me about asking needless questions, I just needed to know how this lady could have gotten assaulted at church. So I asked directly.

"Mmm, mmm, mmm." She responded with a distant look and a slight smile. "You know the part in the wedding where the preacher says 'If anyone has any reason why these two should not be wedded in holy matrimony, speak now or forever hold your peace'? You know that part?"

"I do," I said, recalling the moment in my own wedding years before. "Did you say something?"

"I did," she said raising her chin even higher.

"What did you say?" I realized I had gone too far, but I was into it now.

"I stood up front and told the church that the groom loved me more than he did the bride. And to prove it I told them that he was in my bed last night. That's when I got this," she said pointing to her eye.

"The groom hit you?"

"Nope, the bride," she said.

"What happened then?" I asked slack jawed.

"I knocked her teeth out." She raised her right fist like a boxer. "The groom tried to drag me out of the church by my neck."

"Did they go on with the wedding?" I asked, stifling a laugh. It seemed too wild to be true.

"They tried, but I went around to the open windows on the other side of the church and told everyone that I was having his baby. That's when all hell broke loose." And with that she broke into a pearly smile.

"Man oh man" I exclaimed. "How did it finally end?"

"In the parking lot," she said with a haughty shrug. "Some of the groomsmen are my brothers."

"So that explains all the guys wearing tuxedos in the waiting room," I mused, finally seeing the whole picture.

Stepping out to the nurses' station I got the attention of the charge nurse. "Can you please place the friends of the bride on the left side of the ER and the friends of the groom on the right." She only stared at me. "I just have this thing about proper wedding etiquette."

Since that night, whenever I hear that traditional phrase uttered at a wedding I always hold my breath and take a quick look to my right and left.

43

Square One

AH, JULY ON THE CHESAPEAKE BAY: steamed crabs, sunburns, and sailing. And at the hospital, a fresh crop of interns. Those childlike creatures in starched white jackets that roam through the hospital with wide eyes, spouting long-forgotten medical facts, while asking where the lab is located and how to operate the computers. Don't get me wrong; I love interns. It's just I don't expect to work with them.

I saw him long before he saw me. He stood by the nurses' station, hands in his new lab coat pockets, shifting his weight from one foot to the other. I walked right by unnoticed in shorts, a t-shirt, and a ball cap. It wasn't until I had changed into my usual working attire, rumpled scrubs and lab coat, that he addressed me.

"Dr. Plaster?"

"Uh, that's right." I was trying to ignore him as I grabbed an armload of charts.

"I'm Dave Mandell," he said with a certain uneasiness. "I'm one of the new interns just getting started this month."

"And they put you in the ER?" I thought this was a bad joke on both of us. I looked at the rack overflowing with charts, then back at the intern. "Oh, well," I said with resignation to a long night, "I hope you got your track shoes on. So, how did you like your med school EM rotation?"

"I didn't get to rotate through the ED," he said. "That's why they gave it to me first."

"Really?" I said flatly. This was worse than I thought. This reminded me of the times my wife sent me to the store with a toddler in hand just to punish me. I took a long breath to let the moment pass.

"Why don't you go see a patient; then you can come back and present the case to me. I'll go meet them and do a brief check before signing off." I thumbed through the charts and came up with a couple. The first one said, "Grease burn to hand." *He can't get in too much trouble with this,* I thought. I didn't want him to go stand in the corner, but I really needed to get to work. Our group had recently introduced bonuses based on RVU production. I really didn't need a little helper to slow things to a crawl.

He opened the first chart and stared at the template with its maze of questions. "It's just a bunch of circles and slashes," I said. "You'll get the hang of it pretty quick." I bolted for the first patient as he wandered off, gazing up at the number signs over the ED cubicles.

About two hours later as I was humming through the patients, I realized that I hadn't seen the young doctor again. Finally, as I was heading off to get another armful of charts, he emerged from one of the rooms.

"Can I present my case to you now?" he asked.

"Sure," I said, picking up my pile of charts. "Where's the patient? You can present the case while we walk." I saw the number on the chart before he responded and headed off in a long, quick stride.

"Mr. Granthum is a 55-year-old, married, white male with a twenty pack-year history of smoking. Five hours prior to admission, while deep-frying some chicken, he suffered two burns from grease that splashed on his right dorsal hand. One burn was two-by-two centimeters..." My mind began to wander as he reported every conceivable question that one could ask a person with a minor burn. I was expecting to hear what barbecue sauce the guy was using. He had his head so buried in the chart that he almost hit the edge of the doorframe as we entered the room. The entire chart was covered with circles, slashes, and notes written in the margin.

"Hi, I'm Dr. Plaster," I said, sweeping into the room. The patient was a guy with a deep tan, a strong odor of fried chicken, and two small but obviously painful second-degree burns. "That looks like it hurts."

"Yeah, give me something for the pain so I can get back to the picnic before everyone leaves."

"No problem," I said, as I spun to leave the room. "And leave the blisters until they rupture on their own. They're nature's Band-Aid." Turning to the intern as we left, I spoke in rapid fire. "The things to note about the burn are: first, it's less than one percent of BSA, uh, that is body surface area. Second, it's only partial thickness. And third, it's not circumferential. Cover the wound with an antibacterial dressing and give him an analgesic."

"Don't you want to hear the rest of the presentation?" he asked somewhat deflated.

"I'm sure your exam was thorough," I said, hoping to appease him.

"Where did you read that blisters should be left intact?" he asked, as we raced off to the next room.

"Nowhere," I said. "My mother always told me that. So what's the next patient's problem?"

"Syncope," he said, somewhat out of breath.

"Well, there you go. Have fun," I said over my shoulder as I charged off to the next room. Hours later he caught me between rooms and, without further pause, launched into the next patient's history, physical exam, family history, review of systems, and differential diagnosis. As we stood in the hallway, the perpetual motion of the ED came to a halt. I tried to listen to every word, but I found myself watching him and drifting back to my first July as an intern...

Reporting on a Tuesday, I was issued two pairs of white pants, two white coats, a meal ticket, ID card, and told to report to House Medicine. The service was an anachronism with its large ward of all male patients. It was run by interns and residents with the attending physicians only coming in once a week for grand rounds. Arriving at five in the morning to get sign-out from the last intern, I poured over each chart. But I soon gathered that if he had any idea what was wrong with the patients, his charts certainly didn't show it. I was lost. The first morning rounds featured a rapid-fire series of questions by the chief resident to which each intern shrugged, known in the hospital as the "intern's salute." I hoped against all hopes that the next day would be better.

Not so. The next day while we all stood over a patient on the ward, one of my patients in a nearby bed suddenly gave a loud shout and fell onto the floor moaning and semi-conscious. The entire group raced to him. After a brief examination, the chief turned to the group and asked, "Who has this patient?"

"I do," I mumbled, barely able to speak.

"What's wrong with this patient?" he asked. The entire group stared at me.

"I just got here yesterday, sir," I responded pathetically. The truth was I didn't have a clue what was wrong with this man.

"Maybe he's had a pulmonary embolism," the second-year chimed in, hoping to impress the chief.

"That's it, yeah, maybe he has a PE," I joined, eager for the help.

"OK, then, what should you do?" asked the chief.

"Heparin," I guessed.

"Right, ten thousand unit bolus," he said with authority. And so that's what we did. There was only one problem: the patient didn't have a PE. We had the wrong letters. He'd had a Triple A, an abdominal aortic aneurysm. We all stood in horror as his ruptured aneurysm filled his peritoneum with anti-coagulated blood. I survived the rotation but the patient didn't. I proved I could learn from a mistake, and the patient proved why you shouldn't go into the hospital in July.

Dr. Mandell went on to see a total of four patients during his first twelve-hour shift. Meanwhile I saw almost forty. By the end, we were both completely exhausted.

"How do you do this night after night?" he asked, slumping in a chair. He was a bright kid and his hard work was truly endearing. The truth was he was light years ahead of where I had started.

"You'll do OK," I assured him. "I'll teach you whatever I can. And look at the bright side," I put a collegial hand on his shoulder. "At least you didn't kill anyone."

44

Telemedicine

I WAS JUST SITTING AT THE NURSES' STATION filling out my charts and trying to mind my own business. But I couldn't help overhear one of the nurses tell a person on the phone, "I'm sorry sir, but I can't give you any advice. If you think you have an emergency you can come to the hospital and the doctor will see you."

"Don't tell him that," I whispered somewhat frantically. It was one of my pet peeves. I understand that you can't tell a person with an upset stomach to take Maalox because they might be having a heart attack. But sometimes the diagnosis really is simple and harmless. And telling them to come to the hospital does no good for anyone, especially me. "Let me talk to him," I said, reaching for the phone. The nurse scowled at me as if to say, *You're going to get sued for this! Just wait and see!*

"What can I do for you, sir? I'm the doctor," I said with authority.

"Doctor who?" the nurse whispered, taunting me. I scowled back. I knew better than to give my name. Just in case the nurse was right, I wanted to remain nameless.

"Oh my god, oh my god," the voice on the other end of the line kept saying through heavy breathing. "I can't feel my face or my hands!"

"What happened?" I asked calmly.

"I just had...the best sex...of my entire life," he said with his voice shaking. "And now...I can't feel...anything! I think...I'm going blind!"

"I'm really happy for you, sir" I replied blandly. "But I'm sure you're going to be OK." The nurse was looking at me quizzically. I put my hand over the phone and whispered, "He's had a big orgasm and now he's hyperventilating." Turning back to the patient I said, "Just breathe into a paper bag for a few minutes. I'm sure the symptoms will go away." My previous comment must have been overheard by the nurses because I was now surrounded by a large group of second-guessers.

"He's short of breath after sex. Maybe he's having a heart attack!" the first cautious nurse said.

"He sounds too young," I whispered dismissively.

"How big was his orgasm?" asked a second nurse with a raised eyebrow.

"Who cares about him," snapped another nurse. "Did *she* have an orgasm? He probably doesn't know, or care."

"I wish I could have one," I heard someone say in a mock seductive voice.

"Would all you guys please just give it up!" I growled. "I'm trying to give some sound medical advice here. And besides, what ever happened to patient privacy?"

"HIPPA, schmippa," I heard someone mumble in response. Just then I heard the phone drop to the floor with a loud crack.

"Sir, sir?" I began calling into the phone. "Sir, is everything alright?"

"I told you that you were going to get sued," the first nurse said exultantly. "He's probably lying on the floor dead right now."

"I'm sure you would love that," I said under my breath. "Sir, can you answer the phone?" I was almost shouting into the receiver. "Hello?"

I finally heard a soft female voice on the other line. "Who is this?"

"Uh, this is Dr. Plaster," I blurted, blowing my cover before thinking.

"Dr.? Who?" the woman asked incredulously.

"Uh, yes, this is Dr. Plaster from the emergency room," I said authoritatively.

"This is the emergency room?" She was obviously still wondering what was going on.

"Is your friend alright?" I asked, getting to the point.

"Uh, sure," she said tentatively. "And why did you call us?"

"I didn't call you..."

"And what did you tell him to do?" She was starting to sound a little irritated.

"He called me," I said defensively.

"Did you tell him to put a bag on his head?"

"He put a bag on his head?" I asked lamely. With that statement the entire nursing staff raced back to stand beside me.

"Dr. Plaster told him to put a bag on his head," one of the nurses announced to the group.

"What?" They all gasped.

"I DID NOT!" I shouted over the clamor after covering the receiver.

"I came back from the bathroom," the female voice went on. "And my husband is standing in the middle of the room buck naked with a bag over his head. Did you tell him to do that?" she demanded.

"It's not plastic, is it?" I asked defensively.

"No," she said slowly. "It's a bag from one of our wedding gifts."

"Wedding gifts?" I asked, feeling my stomach sink. "Is this your honeymoon?"

"Yes," she said slowly. "And thanks for ruining a perfectly beautiful evening."

"But I didn't call! He called...I just told him to breathe...Oh well," I said in final exasperation. "Is he OK?"

"Are you OK, baby?" I heard her say in a saccharine sweet voice.

"I'm doing better," I heard a muffled voice say. It sounded like he still had the bag on his head. Then after the sound of paper rustling I heard a full voice: "Oh baby, I love you so much." Then the phone dropped to the floor again with a loud clank.

I couldn't believe it. "I think they're at it again...on the floor," I said to the nurses.

"Can you hear them?" the charge nurse asked.

"Put it on speaker phone," someone shouted.

"I wish my husband could have gone a second round on our honeymoon," I heard another mumble.

"Bunnies," Nurse Birkenstock said disgustingly.

I glared. "Geez, you guys are incorrigible," I said self-righteously hanging up the phone. "We still have patients here you know." I looked around to see the entire staff huddled around the nurses' station. As everyone walked away in a huff I laughed to myself.

The rest of the night went without a hitch. And I didn't take any more calls even though the nurse tried to hand me the phone several times. As I was trudging to the car I got a call on my cell phone.

"Honey," my wife said. "My allergies might be acting up. I've been short of breath all night. What do you think I should do?"

"Just put a bag on your head and I'll be home in a few minutes to take a look," I responded.

"What?" she said sharply. "Listen buster; you better not have said what I think I heard..."

I stifled a chuckle. "I'll explain when I get home."

45

Show Me

IT WAS THE WEE HOURS of the morning when I went to see Jim Hickey. Things had started to slow a bit so I settled down onto the stool to write his history. The patient was a man in his thirties with short-cropped hair and the clothing of a common laborer. While the chart said he was a truck driver for a local construction company, the complexity of his speech made me think of someone with a college education. Although the complaint was minor, I was still required to ask all the usual questions about past medical problems. That's when he caught my attention.

"Have you ever had any significant medical problems in the past?" I asked with my pen poised over the negative box.

"Yes," he explained. "I used to have PNH."

I looked up from the chart. "Are you talking about paroxysmal nocturnal hemoglobinuria?"

"Yes, it was diagnosed when I was a teenager," he said without expression.

"I was having dark urine in the morning and feeling really tired. My family doctor found that my blood count was really low. Initially he thought I had blood in my urine, and that that's why I was anemic. But it turned out that I just had the hemoglobin part of my blood in my urine. Something was making the red blood cells break apart. He didn't know what it was so he sent me to a specialist at a big hospital. That's where they made the diagnosis."

"That's a pretty rare disorder." I actually didn't remember much about the disorder except that it was one of the rare things that caused hemoglobin in the urine. I remembered it from studying for the boards. I remembered it being called the 'great impersonator.'

"Yeah, the hematologist said I was one in a million."

"You 'used' to have it?" I asked. "I thought, except for possibly stem cell transplantation, there wasn't any cure for the disorder."

"That's right."

"Oh, so you received a stem cell transplant?" I turned back to the chart. "That's cool. When and where did that happen?"

"No, I didn't do that," he said.

I paused. "So, you're still getting periodic transfusions?"

"No, not anymore," he said. It seemed he was being evasive.

"So how did they treat you?" I asked. "I remotely remember reading something about some drug that costs over a half million dollars a year.... Did you get that?" I was really scraping the bottom of my memory.

"No, I got blood transfusions almost every month for nearly ten years," he said with remote detachment. "They said that most people didn't live much longer than that with this disease. The hematologist warned me that I was a high risk to develop blood clots. He said that they used to think that you got it from something, but now they think it's a genetic thing."

"I did read something about that. So what happened?" I stopped taking notes and was genuinely curious. "Are you still getting transfusions?"

"Oh no," he said with a slight smile. "I haven't had a transfusion in about five years."

"Really. How did your doctors cure you?"

"My doctors didn't cure me," he said. "I was healed."

"Oh...really?" I said skeptically.

"Yep," he said with a slight shrug. I studied his face to see if there was any sign that he was making this up. From time to time I've run into people with Munchhausen's Syndrome, where they make up symptoms just for the attention. But this guy didn't look like that.

"Do you mind explaining *how* you were healed?" I asked.

"Do you really want to hear this?" he said softly. He leaned forward and looked me in the eyes. It was like he was reading my mind and I was embarrassed that he had seen right through my false objectivity.

"Yes," I said with less prejudice.

"Well," he paused for a moment. "After several years of monthly blood transfusions they said that my kidneys were in jeopardy of failing and my spleen was going to rupture. They told me I needed a bone marrow transplant to live. They said I had plastic anemia."

"Oh, OK," I said nodding my head. *Maybe he's not nuts, just ignorant.* I felt somewhat relieved. *I guess he just saw the bone marrow donor as his savior rather than the doctors.* "So the bone marrow worked?" I dropped my head to begin writing in the PMH block again.

"No," he replied. "I didn't have the bone marrow."

"And why not?" The tone of my voice was clearly inquisitional.

"Do you really want to hear this?" he questioned again. I could tell this was personal for him and that he was not about to have his integrity questioned.

"Yes," I responded, coming back to a respectful tone.

"It was the night before I was to receive my bone marrow transplant." He looked at me. "And God told me I didn't need to have it because I was healed."

At first I didn't know what to say. "What did God's voice sound like?" I finally asked. I had used this question before with others who had 'heard

God' and the voice was usually that of a long lost mother or father. My next question was going to be 'Have you ever seen a psychiatrist?'

"It wasn't really like a human voice," he said breaking into my clinical assessment. "In fact, it wasn't really a voice, if you know what I mean. But it was unmistakable. It had to be God."

I gave a forced smile, nodding my head mechanically. *'If you know what I mean.'* My rational mind finally interrupted. *Uh, no! I don't know what you mean. So why am I nodding my head?*

We were at a stalemate. He was not apparently psychotic, nor did he have a psych history. But this was one of the strangest stories I'd ever heard. I sat staring at him. "And you were healed?"

"Yep," he said with some resignation. "I didn't think you would believe me. Go check it out. All my records are here."

The charge nurse opened the door and saw my bewildered expression. Without saying a word she stepped in carrying five charts with a look that read *Where've you been for the last hour?* I snapped back to reality. Finishing the chart without commenting on his history, I handed it to the nurse. Grabbing the armload from her I headed out the door.

"Well, was he telling the truth?" my wife asked on hearing the story after my arrival home.

"That's the strange thing about it," I said between mouthfuls of breakfast. "I chased down his records. He had transfusions every month or so for all the years he said. And then they suddenly stop, exactly when he said. Now his counts are fine. I'll be damned if his records didn't bear out every word."

"Don't use language like that around this house," she glared. "You might just get your wish. But you still don't believe him, do you?"

"I'm sorry for the swearing," I said. "But do you really believe he was healed? He probably had a spontaneous remission. They happen you know. I looked it up. I'm a scientist, for crying out loud. I need to know *how* things happen for me to believe in them. You know my motto: 'I'm from Missouri, you'll have to show me.'"

"I thought he did," she said, pouring the coffee. There was a long silence. I was at the same stalemate again. Finally she walked over and sat down at the table, challenging me to look in her eyes. "And have you ever wondered *how* I could love you all these years?"

I looked up and saw her smiling. She had me there.

46

History Lesson

I LOVE IT WHEN THE LECTURERS SAY the same thing: "Take a good history..." They act as if we don't know what questions to ask. Don't they get it? The right questions are written on the template. But sometimes I just didn't know what to do with what the patient told me. Let me give you an example.

"Hi, I'm Dr. Plaster. What brings you to the emergency department tonight?"

The patient on the bed gave an empty look. "She dahsn't speak English," said a woman sitting disinterestedly at bedside eating peanut butter crackers and drinking a soda. "She's from Cahm-ah-rooon."

"That's cool," I said. "Are you a relative?"

"No," she said, ignoring me and looking around the room.

So much for the open-ended question technique, I thought. "Where does your stomach hurt?" I asked. Somehow the triage nurse had learned that the patient's problem was abdominal pain. The woman sitting by the bed spoke with her friend for a few minutes, then turned back to me.

"All over."

"Up here, down there, where?" I pointed to the different quadrants. The ladies talked for several minutes more with the patient rubbing all over her abdomen and groaning.

"Up there," said the woman pointing in the general region of her friend.

"Up here?" I asked, pointing to her stomach region.

"No."

"Here?" pointing to the gall bladder region.

"No."

"Here?" poking the belly button.

"No."

"Well, where then?"

They spoke for a few more minutes. "Here," she finally said, pointing to the left lower quadrant.

"I thought you said 'up there.'"

"That's right."

OK, I thought. *At least I know it's left lower quadrant pain.* "How long has it been going on?"

The ladies talked some more. "A while."

"A long while or a short while?"

"A short while."

"Just how long is a 'short while?'" I asked, thinking myself clever.

"Since her mother died," the woman said with a sorrowful look.

"I'm sorry to hear that," I responded. "How long ago did her mother die?"

"A while." This time her words seemed to have a different upward inflection. Maybe it was longer than I thought...

"What does the pain feel like?" I asked, working down the template.

They talked for several more minutes. "She says it feels like her stomach is talking to her."

I took off my glasses and rubbed my face. "What does her stomach say?" I continued. *Is it the voice of your mother telling you to clean your room, or is it the dog telling you to kill the neighbors?* Now I was hearing voices. Both women were looking at me blankly when I'd returned from my internal conversation. "Is there anything that seems to make it better or worse?" I asked, reading further down the template.

"The television," the interpreter said after questioning her friend.

Does watching TV make it better or does EATING THE TV MAKE IT WORSE??? My face was getting red. *Oh, wait a second!* My eye caught sight of a box next to a phrase at the beginning of the chart.

"Unable to obtain history due to_____." *Well that does it. The history is unobtainable because: a) the patient is a moron, b) the interpreter is a moron, or c) the doctor is a moron.* I shook my head. I seemed to be having an out-of-body experience. Despite all this I attempted a review of systems.

The physical exam wasn't much better. Everything appeared normal until I tried to palpate her left lower quadrant. Then the patient grabbed my hand and moaned. Her friend looked at me as though I was attempting to violate her.

A professor of mine in medical school used to say, "The diagnosis is made by the history and confirmed by the physical exam. Only the weak clinician needs the lab to make a diagnosis." Well, I'll admit it; that night I was a weak clinician. I ordered a CT scan as well as every blood and urine test I could think of. At the very least they would allow me some time to get away and reflect on the situation.

When all the results had come back she had a normal urine, negative pregnancy test, slightly high white count, and a non-diagnostic CT. I called the surgery resident.

"I've got a hot abdomen down here that you need to see and admit," I said with some authority over the phone.

"How bad is it?"

"Oh, real bad," I warned.

"Does she need surgery tonight?"

"Well, I wouldn't want to tell you how to do your business," I demurred.

My partner watched with begrudging admiration as I kicked an air-football. "Were you able to punt that case to surgery?" he asked.

"Look at the hang time on that baby," I said, doing a little end-zone dance. But before I could even pick up another chart the surgery intern appeared.

My partner grinned. "Five bucks says that the case will be back in your lap before the end of the shift," he goaded.

Picking up several charts, I hoped to avoid the intern by hiding in the patients' rooms. I chuckled to myself when I glanced over and saw him listening intently to the interpreter. *He's Korean and she's Cameroonian; he won't get past her name.*

After an hour I was sure that the coast was clear and returned to the nurses' station. But just when I thought the patient had been taken upstairs, I saw the intern come out of the room and walk over to me.

"Wow, you are quite a clinician, Dr. Plaster," he said sincerely. "I would have never gotten that diagnosis from her history and physical. How did you discover that she had intermittent sigmoid volvulus?"

"Uh...um...well," I paused and took a deep breath.

"I didn't even think of it until she showed me her medical records from the Mayo Clinic."

"She had..." I stopped myself.

"We'll admit her to our service for observation, just in case she needs surgery. Great case!" The intern insisted before exiting the room.

"Great case," my partner mocked.

"How was I supposed to know she had a previous workup? Besides that was on my differential too, just a little further down the list," I mumbled as he walked away. "I knew she was sick," I called out to him.

After my shift I returned home to find my wife in high gear. "I need for you to take out the trash; it's piling up in the mud room and starting to smell.

And take the van to the service station for an oil change."

"Hey, what happened to 'Hi honey, how was your night?'" I attempted my best June Cleaver imitation.

"Get your sleep, but when you get up I have some things for you to do. You need to start pulling your weight around here, buddy." It was obvious that she had been stewing on this all night. "How long has it been since you took out the trash, huh?"

"A while," I sighed. "A short while."

47

Conspiracy Theory

"YOU WON'T BELIEVE WHAT MY LAST PATIENT told me," the evening doc said as he was signing out. "The patient was a twelve-year-old girl with belly pain," he began explaining. "I asked her about everything possible, but nothing was coming up positive. Finally in desperation I asked her mother 'Do you think it's possible that your daughter has ever had sexual intercourse?' The mother looks at me and says, 'Whaal,'" he imitated her drawl. "'Ah don't know 'bout anythang like that. But if you thank she needs it, you go rat ahead and geeve it to her. Cuz we got the health card and it'll pay fer it.'"

While it was comical to hear about this woman's misunderstanding, the sense of entitlement in the health care system is hard to laugh at. I've often told people that beds in the ED are like airline seats: some people pay a lot while others pay very little. That's why we refer to some of our regular patients as frequent flyers. But I must confess that over the years it's been a struggle for me, feeling like a slave to this sense of entitlement.

"Don't forget that we have an appointment with the accountant after you get home from your shift tomorrow," my wife said cheerily as I headed out the door in my scrubs. It was the end of the year and time to get the "good news, bad news" speech from the accountant.

"It looks like you've had a very good year," he said brightly as I slumped at one end of the oversized conference table. "You're a lucky man."

"I know," I said gloomily. Despite still having my scrubs and lab coat on, it felt like I was sitting in a cold examining room wearing a paper gown waiting to get a freezing sigmoidoscope.

"You know what that means?" he said looking over his spectacles.

"I know." I sighed deeply.

"Even though you've paid a lot already, you're still going to owe a bundle on this year's taxes."

I shook my head. "I saw an EZ IRS short form once that looked very official," I recounted numbly. "It just had two lines. Line one asked for 'Total earnings for this tax year.' Line two just said 'Send it in.'"

"That's pretty funny," he chuckled.

"Yeah, if it wasn't true. And you know the hard part about this?" I sat up, starting to bristle. "I see where all this money is going. It's going to pay for all the bogus medical problems that I see every night."

"Well at least it's coming back to you," he said philosophically.

"Let's see how this works." I was wide awake now. "First I have to work all night and see every person who shows up regardless of whether they pay or not. Then I pay an accountant God knows what (no offense) to figure out how much I owe the government." Out of the corner of my eye I caught my wife scowling. "Then I have to argue with the pinheads at the IRS about whether it's the right amount. Then Congress has the gall to decide what tiny fraction of my money they'll give back to me for working all night to see every patient. Somethin' ain't right about that," I said, imitating my old grandpa.

"He's tired," my wife smiled warily at the accountant. "We'll talk about this later," she whispered to me.

"It's not like I don't want to help those poor ignorant souls that I see every night," I protested to my wife as we walked to the car. "I do. But I hate it that they act like I owe it to them. What happened to the good ole days when the doc would say to the poor farmer 'Just pay me when you can'. Or maybe, 'I know you're on hard times now, so don't worry about paying me. Consider this visit a gift.' Even if they couldn't pay, at least they knew they owed something for their care. Now they act like I owe them! Health care is not a right!"

"Calm down," she chided me. "It's not like all your patients are narcissistic ignoramuses. Besides, are you ranting because the taxes are too high or because a few of your patients don't show enough gratitude?"

Her analysis gave me pause for thought. "It's both," I said, now more in control. "Don't you see how they're related? When patients have a 'right' to have someone else take care of their every need, somebody has to pay for it. Then the government steps in and offers to 'pay for everything.'" I was exaggerating each phrase for dramatic effect. "But then where does the government go to get the money to pay for all their benevolence? Me!"

"Everyone should be as oppressed as we are." She stopped the conversation with a little signal that she used frequently. It was her index finger rubbing back and forth across her thumb. I made the mistake once, in the middle of an argument, of asking what she was doing. "I'm playing on the world's smallest violin, *My Heart Bleeds for You,*" she told me.

We went home and I finally got some sleep. But I dreamed fitfully of poor farmers lining up outside the ED, each one approaching me and saying, 'Thank you doctor, you saved my life. I can't pay you so I brought you this chicken.' In my dream there were thousands of chickens everywhere, clucking and crapping on everything. It was horrible.

And wouldn't you know it, throughout the entire weekend everyone around me was saying 'thank you' for the slightest courtesy. I was beginning to feel like a spoiled brat. When it came time to go to church at the Naval Academy chapel on Sunday, I was ready to repent of my sinful attitude and get right with God. That was until the chaplain got up to speak.

"Don't do your good deeds so people will see you and praise you. You'll have your reward. Do your good deeds in secret, then your Father in heaven will see and reward you."

"Hey," I whispered to my wife. "Is he saying I shouldn't be looking for people to say thanks?"

"Shh!" She could see I was starting to get agitated again. "We can talk about this after church."

"Oh, I get it," I said louder. "I can see what this is all about." People started to glance my way as my wife began to glare. "He's telling me to just do my job and shut up about being thanked for it."

"That's right," she scowled, "shut up!"

"Jesus said," the chaplain continued, 'If someone wants to sue you and take your tunic, let him have your cloak as well."

"Now he's using Jesus to justify the IRS using and abusing me. That's just not right." When the collection plate was passed I was studying the wad of cash in my wallet for how much to give. My wife grabbed my wallet and counted out twice as much as I had planned. Now it was my turn to glare.

As we filed out of the church my wife tried to ignore my continuing rant. "I wish I could stand by the door after every shift and have everyone thank me." Approaching the smiling chaplain I stuck out my hand. "All I want to know is, did the IRS tell you to preach that sermon?"

Totally bewildered he looked to my wife. "He's been working nights, and he's a little tired," she said pulling me out the door.

48

Aphephobia

I ONCE KNEW AN EMERGENCY PHYSICIAN who would do anything he could to avoid touching his patients. It wasn't that he was afraid of getting or giving an infectious disease. It seemed to go much deeper than that. Even when infection was not at issue, such as when he palpated a patient's anterior abdomen, he would carefully cover the patient's skin with a Kleenex so that there would be no direct contact. I think he left emergency medicine and went on to a radiology residency where he could sit alone in a dark room never seeing, let alone touching, a real human being.

I don't say this in criticism. Emergency medicine just wasn't a good fit for him. Real emergency physicians can't be afraid to touch their patients, head to toe, inside and out, clean or dirty. This is not a specialty for the squeamish. Nor do I mean to say that I ignore universal precautions. I wear a mask, gloves, and gowns any and every time that they are indicated. What I'm getting at is the tendency to stand off and examine the patient from afar.

Not literally from afar (though I did know a physician once who would shine his flashlight from across the room to look into his patient's throats): I'm talking about examining a patient from the standpoint of detachment.

In certain areas of the Middle East, there is such a premium on modesty that a physician is not allowed to see his patients except through a small hole in a blanket that is hung between them. He never sees the whole patient and is barely able to touch the patient at all.

American doctors face challenges similar to their Middle Eastern counterparts, but they're expressed in a very different manner. The patient is totally disrobed but we may never really see them. Very efficient systems triage patients according to a standard form with standard questions. "Score your pain from one to ten," we ask. According to the answers we can offer a standard set of labs and x-rays. The doctor will confirm the information on the forms, perform a cursory exam, look at the labs and x-rays, and dispose of the patient using either a standard set of admission orders or a pre-printed set of home-going instructions. The end result is a well-documented chart than can withstand the assault of the most tenacious lawyer while also pleasing the administration by capturing all the possible charges. But the system can also cause the physician to miss seeing the whole patient.

"Of course I touch the patients," my colleagues say when challenged on the point. "I look into their throats, feel their necks, listen to their chests." And I'm sure that's true. We all have to feel and probe and prick and touch our patients. And that touching is sometimes not very pleasant, for us or for them. So we even train ourselves to be somewhat detached. When I was a young physician with sweaty palms and a racing heart I used to tell myself, *If I care too much about hurting the patient, I won't be able to do what I need to do.* And there may have been an element of truth in that. But that sort of detachment may also lead to missing a fundamental aspect of the relationship between the doctor and the patient.

I once knew a doctor who would hold a patient's hand when speaking to them, particularly the very sick and dying. And not just a long handshake;

he would stand at the bedside and hold their hand. I've even seen him stroke a patient's hair. That may seem too intimate but it beats what I've done many times, which is to sit across the room with my head buried in the chart, asking questions and scribbling notes. I'll bet at the end of the encounter my friend knew a lot more about his patient than I did mine.

And his physical exam went the same way. He had developed a fine touch by closely observing the details of every exam. His exam was slow and gentle, analyzing the patient's slightest reaction to his probing. He relied on fewer lab tests and x-rays. He could diagnose appendicitis with similar accuracy to CT, without all the radiation. Of course he wasn't perfect; but when he was wrong he had such a relationship with the patient that they seldom considered blaming him, much less suing. They seemed to see him as a friend and not just a technician.

Even more than getting a better diagnosis, touching goes a long way toward starting the healing process. When a patient would tell my mentor about something that was painful or worrisome, he would reach out and take a hand or shoulder and say something like "I'm really sorry. That sounds like it really hurts." I know that sounds hokey, but he really meant it and the patient knew so.

I can just see my colleagues rolling their eyes as they assume that this guy was an easy mark for any patient looking for a little sympathy and a lot of narcotics. But he wasn't. He seldom wrote for big time analgesics. He didn't have to prove he cared by giving inappropriate doses of opiates. If he thought narcotics addiction was a potential problem, he would say so to the patient. And he meant it! He wasn't just disgusted with the junkies; he really cared for them and didn't want to hurt them further. And believe it or not, they usually understood.

Some people have tried to make touching patients into a science itself. It's called touch therapy. It's actually a variant of Chinese medicine called chi dong. The practitioners believe that, because the body gives off some kind of energy, they can treat a patient by passing their hands over an injured area.

It seems to be an attempt to 'touch' the patient without actually touching them. And believe it or not, some hospitals are actually providing this as a therapeutic modality.

But science has a way of taking the humanity out of everything. If listening is nothing more than interpreting the sounds that a patient makes, caregivers will eventually be replaced by speech-recognition programs. And if touching is no more than coordinating energy waves that are interpreted by our electro-neural pathways, we will be replaced by some sort of super-sensitive scanner. But this will only happen if we allow it, if we lose the very skills that make us indispensable.

It's true that when my next patient comes in with cardiac arrest I'll need to know the chemistry and physics, the anatomy and physiology, to get that heart started again. But that is not all there is to being an emergency physician. I'll need to hold the hands, dry the eyes, or hold up his wife as she walks to his room. I'll need to touch and care for the hearts of my own team, who put everything on the line to save a life. As much as I might like to stay on one side of the room and see life through a hole in a blanket, I cannot. As painful and messy as it might be, for the patient and for myself, I must touch the patient.

ACKNOWLEDGMENTS

I HAVE TO ADMIT THAT, EVEN AFTER twenty years of collecting stories, this book would never have come to completion without the dedicated work of Eli Moore. His organizational skills, his editing, and his encouragement were boundless and invaluable resources. Many thanks, as well, to Emily DeBusk for her detailed copyediting; she helped a group of stories come together in the form of a book. I'm very grateful to Elise Grinstead for the quality of her creative design with the page layout. My deep gratitude and appreciation go to my son Logan Plaster who has designed the cover and done the difficult job of honing my writing skills for so many of my stories. I also want to thank Graham, my oldest son, for his example of service and sacrifice that inspired me to follow in his footsteps and join the Navy. And last, my heartfelt thanks go to my dearest and only daughter, Whitney Plaster Landon, who grew up in this book. She inspired me to tell these stories for all the children of emergency physicians who watch their mothers or fathers trudge off to the hospital every night, only to return sleepy-eyed and weary as they, the kids, dash off to school.